MW00910980

# Yours, Truly

## A Novel by
## Crystal White

Hope
Freelancing
Kansas City

Editor: Sarah Cicconetti
Senior Editor: Danielle Bergey

Published in Kansas City by Hope Freelancing.
www.hopefreelancing.com

Cover design by Ian Stotts
Interior design by Danielle Bergey

Crystal White
www.shininglikeyou.com
shinelikeyou@yahoo.com


ISBN-13: 978-0-9888200-0-5
ISBN-10: 098882000

Printed in the United States of America.

# Dedication

*I want to dedicate this book to Jesus and thank Him for giving me the gift to write. I not only thank You for giving me this gift but for showing me how to use this gift, for the benefit of others.*

*I want to dedicate this book to my husband Anthony and our son Anthony, Jr.*

*Last but not least I want to dedicate this book to every person who will read this story and be inspired to seek their own purpose. There is no need to compare yourself to others. You have been created uniquely for such a time as this. Forgiveness and patience will reap you a harvest of blessings.*

# One

The car ride home was silent for the most part. I was looking out the window when my Dad said, "I can't believe they didn't pick you baby, I thought those pictures we gave them were beautiful."

"I am not surprised," my momma commented.

"Pamela, why would you say that?" my dad asked.

"Well, I wasn't saying it to be mean, but I keep telling Truly she could stand to lose a few more pounds if she wants to make it in the entertainment industry." She turned around looking at me. "You know I can give you this dieting book I just finished."

"Yeah, I'll take a look at it," I mumbled to try to get her off the subject quickly.

Turning around, Momma continued, "If Truly gets down to, or close to, the size of Vanessa, she will be able to be successful entertaining people."

I looked at my sister, but she didn't say anything. She was just staring out the window; every now and then glancing at her phone to change a song.

My sister Vanessa is twenty-five, two years older than me. She wins everything. She won the beauty pageant when we were eight and ten years old. She won the singing contest when we were in middle school. She even beat me racing in the backyard when all our cousins would come over and play; Vanessa always beat me. My parents always seemed to notice when *she* won, especially my mom.

My mom and dad continued to argue up until we pulled into our driveway. They argued about why I didn't get chosen for the photo shoot for the upcoming fall edition for Bailey's, a trendy fashion store looking for brochure models. It was well into the summer, late July. Typically, people my sister's and my age were out on their own, not us. We were in search of fame in the name of our mother.

All our lives it seemed like we competed against one another. It is my belief that my sister and I aren't as close as we should be because of this. It seems that my mother is always the judge of our competitions. I always think my mother meant well, but at one point, it made me question if she loved Vanessa more than me. Sometimes the competitions were fun, other times not so much—at least for me.

My sister and I stay with our parents in a suburb of Kansas City. My father is a college professor at a technical school. He is really smart; he even wrote the textbook that he is teaching his class from this semester. My dad is awesome.

My mother, she stays home. I don't know why she does. My sister and I are clearly old enough to change our own diapers. She sells makeup on the side. I think she does it so she can have other people to boss around when my sister and I aren't home.

My parents won't let my sister and I move out of the house until we both get married. My dad says that he wants to know that we are well taken care of. He wants us to save our money and use it to buy a house in the future. Have I said how much I love my Dad?

My sister already has the upper hand on me with savings because she does a lot of modeling jobs on the side. Me, on the other hand, I ask people, "Do you want some flavor in your double espresso?"

After we got home, Mom started preparing dinner. She wanted to celebrate Vanessa's new contract. I grabbed my purse on my way out the front door before I realized that I left my keys in my room. After getting them, with my hand on the doorknob, Mom stopped me, saying, "Uh-uh, where do you think you are going? We're here to celebrate your sister getting the job with Bailey's. I cooked tofu parmigiana."

My dad, sister, and mother were all looking at me as my mom placed the salad bowl in the center of the table.

"I am covering for Casey tonight" I said. "A piece of her work was displayed at the art gallery and she had to be there. I told you that early today on our way home from the photo shoot."

"Yes, you did honey. See you later and be safe. We'll put you some food aside," Dad said.

Mom slowly sat down at the head of the table and watched me scurry out the door.

Since it was Friday night, there were college students and middle-aged folks filling up the coffeehouse. As popular as coffeehouses have become in the last ten years, I've never understood why they make them so small. People were spilling out of the front door like the jelly out of the donut I was shoving in a bag for a customer.

Eleven o'clock felt like it took eternity to arrive. My feet ached as I pushed the mop back and forth. I raised my head to look up at the next area my mop was going to cover, I realized I was at the bulletin board. There was a fluorescent yellow piece of paper with black print that caught my eye:

*Academy Dance*
*New Season Starting*
*Audition for Fall & Winter Performance*
*Try-outs*
*Saturday, August 5, 2011, 6:00 p.m.*
*Downtown Overland Park, KS*

"Hey Truly, what ya staring at?" Jeremy asked. "We're pretty much done back here; we're just waiting for you to get the back of the counter and we can get outta here. You wanna go, or you wanna stay and daydream?" He had a smirk on his face.

Jeremy has been managing this coffeehouse for about seven years. He has been talking about opening his own shop the two years I've been here. So much, that when he mentions his own shop, everyone looks at each other and says, "He's not going anywhere."

"I wanna go. I was just waiting on ya'll to get done in the back," I lied. I ran to the counter and ripped a piece of register tape from the cash register, felt in my apron for a pen, then wrote down the information from the flyer. I crammed the paper and pen into my apron, dragging the big, wet mop to finish slopping the floor with dirty water.

It was two weeks before the Academy Dance audition and one week before Vanessa's Bailey's photo shoot. I had heard of Academy Dance before, but never paid it much attention. For some reason, the fluorescent flyer intrigued me.

I was lying in my bed on a cool Tuesday afternoon. I grabbed my laptop to take a look at the website just to familiarize myself with exactly what happens at Academy Dance. There were beautiful people all over the website; snapshots of men and women dancing; and a tab for upcoming events, which I clicked next. Another page came up with several links to events happening the remainder of the year. I went to the month of August and clicked again. I saw the event that was on the yellow flier. There was a picture of a man and a woman embracing one another like a bride and groom do during their first dance. It read:

"Looking for a ballerina to perform a *pas de deux* at

our 3<sup>rd</sup> annual charity event for cancer research this win-
ter. Auditions for this event and other performances on
Saturday, August 5, 2011—6:00 p.m. at Academy
Dance, Downtown Overland Park, KS."

I rolled over and pondered what I just read. I lay staring at the big red numbers on my table clock, which read
12:00 p.m. I decided I would take a drive to Academy
Dance.

It took about fifteen minutes to get into Downtown
Overland Park. I always loved the downtown areas of
small cities. The buildings are always really small and
the shops are unique. In areas like this, customers are
the main focus, assisting them in finding what they are
looking for, instead of just stocking a whole bunch of
inventory. There is a personal feel to downtown areas
that I just adore.

After finding a free parking space a few blocks away,
I pulled open the door to Academy Dance. I looked
around and the first thing I saw was a room with mirrors
all around a dance floor. There was a small hallway
leading to the front desk. As I made my way down the
hallway, there were hanging pictures of different dance
groups from many years before. There were pictures of
teams dating all the way back to 1979. It was very in-
triguing to see how people and hairstyles have changed
over the years.

As I was staring at this one lady's beehive from '79
who had the title of "Director" under her name, a

woman who sounded mid-thirties said, "Can I help you?" I looked up and made eye contact with her. She was standing next to me with the most pleasant smile on her face. She was a pale-faced woman with blush that made her cheeks a rosy pink color. Although she had sounded young and was very beautiful, she looked forty-five.

"Uh-oh, I was just looking," I said, not sure if I had done anything wrong.

She said, "That is Sarah Cote," pointing to the lady with the beehive. "She's the one who started all of this you see here."

She waved her hand like a genie granting a wish. Then she asked again, "So how can I help you?"

"Well, nothing. I mean, yes. Well, no, not exactly… I was just looking," I finally answered.

"If you follow me I can give you a tour of the place, if you want," she offered.

"Sure, I would love to see the place."

I let out a sigh of relief as I passed the wall and saw the picture of the lady in front of me. She was an African-American woman. Under her picture said, "Lily Brown, Director, 2002-."

I followed her down the narrow hallway where we stopped at the front desk.

"How rude of me, I haven't even introduced myself. I am Lily Brown. I am the Director, as well as a Ballet Master, here at Academy Dance."

I smiled and shook her hand as if it was my first time knowing that.

"My name is Truly Michaels."

"Nice to meet you Truly," she said.

Lily took me back into an office where there was a collage of pictures and plaques hanging all around the room. She also showed me where the restrooms were. After we both took a break to freshen up, she asked me if I would like to see the costume room. Lily led me back to the front desk. There was a door to the left of that, and when she opened it, I saw an emergency exit door at the end of a short hallway. She veered to the right where there was a huge room of costumes. Across the hall, there was another dance room where a man in the middle of the floor was dancing!

Lily didn't notice that I wasn't behind her, and she kept right on into the costume room. My body was frozen and my eyes were locked on this handsome man in the opposite room, "OMG! Only if he could be my 'Beanie'," I said with my mouth hanging open.

He was into whatever he was doing, and it was beautiful. The moves he was doing—I'd never seen such art in dancing until then. His legs were long like paint brushes, stroking the canvas of the air with his elegant moves. I never knew a man could dance with such grace.

His eyes were closed, and he was focused until he lifted his head and saw me looking at him. We were both staring at each other. I was looking at his back

14

while he was staring at me through the mirrors in front of him.

"I-I am so sorry, I didn't mean to disturb you. I-I was just—" I stuttered. This was the second time today I was caught without an explanation.

"Sooo... what were you doing?" he asked. He grabbed a small towel off the back of a chair. He started slowly walking towards me. I got a glimpse of his full figure. This unknown, beautiful man stood 6'1" and looked about 160 pounds. He was black, his skin a honey brown tone, his voice very deep. His hair was cut low, and he had muscles that were not huge, but defined, or what they say when a man is "cut." It was enough for my liking.

Lily came in behind me, and I felt sandwiched between the two of them.

"Where have you been? I was just in there talking away and you weren't even behind me," she said.

"You know this young lady?" he asked Lily.

"Well I just met her today and I was giving her a tour of the place. At least I thought I was," she chuckled.

"My momma loves this place." He turned to Lily. "She probably just walked in with a question and you gave her a tour, huh?"

I looked at the both of them. "Momma?" I felt even more embarrassed that I was crushing on this woman's son.

It seemed as if she had just read my mind and answered, "Yes, this is my son, Mark Brown. Mark, this is Truly," she said as we shook hands. "So, this is your mother. I see the resemblance."

"Yes, but her true resemblance is beauty." He said to his mother while kissing her on the cheek.

I watched him pull away from his mother as he stood tall and strong. My eyes looked up and down along the structure of his face. I noticed his bright white teeth and beautiful pink colored lips as he dabbed at the sweat on his face with the towel. *Look at his perfect skin,* I thought.

Lily and I finally made our way to the costume room while Mark disappeared somewhere. There were all kinds of things in there. Some costumes from the medieval times, a witch's hat and broom, and even some costumes I would consider wild.

I sat around chatting with Lily until some people started trickling into the building. She informed me that her two o' clock class was showing up and invited me to stay and watch. I agreed, but only to stay for a little while because I had to go to work later on in the evening.

I watched as the ballerinas practiced what I heard Lily call *entrechat*. They first watched as she jumped into the air, crossing her legs two times. Then they all followed her lead as she gave them the count.

After about twenty-five minutes into her practice, I waved a silent good-bye to Lily as I left for work. The three-block walk to the car felt great as I told myself, "I'm going to do it. I'm going to audition for the *pas de deux*."

Tuesday nights are typically the slow nights. On these nights Casey and I usually jump onto our phones when Jeremy isn't looking and watch videos on the internet. This night in particular, I pulled up some videos of ballet performances.

"Not on my clock!" I heard a voice behind me shout. I kept watching the video and replied, "You know you sound just like Jeremy, Casey. And you would have gotten me, but I just said 'good-bye' to Jeremy. He decided to go home early since it was slow. He's opening in the morning and wanted to get some rest. Nice try."

"Ah. Jeremy already left. He didn't say good-bye to me. What ya' looking at?" She asked.

"Some ballet performances," I replied.

"Okay!" She said excitedly. "Are you thinking about pulling out the old ballet shoes?"

Casey is my girl. It's been that way since ninth grade. We started hanging in high school when both of us discovered that we didn't care what people thought about us. We both have older sisters who we went to high school with, except Casey also has an older brother. Her older sister was in the marching band at our school and her brother was on the football team. My sister Vanessa was on the dance team. Both of our mothers used to sit behind us at football games and chastise us for not being involved in the school activities. We both liked to sit in the bleachers and watch her brother play football, her sister play in the band, and my sister dance to the beat of the drum during half-time. That's how we met, actually. She was sitting beside her mother while I was sitting in front of mine. When the game was over, we made eye contact with each other while we were waiting for our siblings to come out of the locker rooms. We've been inseparable since.

Casey's mother and father are a replica of mine. But the difference between Casey and me is that she had the guts to get out of there. Casey's mother banned her from getting another tattoo, so she didn't put up any arguments; she just got a newspaper and found an apartment three weeks later. She has now been on her own for a year and is paying her way through art school.

"Yes, I want to try out for Academy Dance's *pas de deux* for their winter charity event," I said.

"I know what Academy Dance is, but remind me what *pas de deux* is again?"

"It is French. It's pretty much when a man and a woman dance a passionate ballet," I explained.

"So, who's the man? That's the real question," she grinned.

"I don't know. I'm not doing it for 'the man.' I'm doing it for me. I'm ready to define myself. I have a background in dance, as you know. The only reason why I didn't continue is because we moved. My dad told me if

I wanted to continue, he would find a company in Kansas for me to dance with. I showed no interest once he brought it up after we moved here. I guess I tried to punish him for making us move for his job by pretending to not want to dance. But I ended up only punishing myself."

"I do remember that one day you pulled out those old shoes at your house , but I mean seriously. I can't imagine you putting some tights and a tutu on now."

"Yeah. I danced from the age of four until eighth grade. Then we moved here when I was going into high school." Silence filled the air as Casey looked at me staring off into space as if my past were playing in front of me like a movie.

"So, who would you say you are now?" Casey asked.

I looked at her, not sure of the question, "What do you mean 'who do I say I am now?'" I asked.

Casey pointed to herself, "I'm an artist. I am currently enrolled in art school. I plan on creating wonderful art that people will someday hang on their walls. You, on the other hand, tend to live in the past. You talk about what was, not about what's to come. So I'm curious, who do you say you are now?"

I sat there, offended that Casey confronted me like that. But more offended at myself because I couldn't answer her question. Casey broke the silence, "Well the great thing is now we have each other, right?" She opened her arms wide enough to hug a bear.

"Right," I said, and filled the space between her arms.

"So, since we are homies, I need you to support me on that day. I want you to come to the auditions with me. We both need to make sure we have that day off," I said.

Eleven o' clock came around once again and we did our routine to shut down the shop. We hugged and said our good-byes before departing. This was the second time in one day I was taking a walk back to my car. But this time I was feeling really confused. *Who am I?*

# Two

Vanessa's shoot with Bailey's went really well. I have to admit that she does have a gift for modeling. She put the clothes on that they provided and went at it. She was a natural in front of the camera.

My mother was there talking to the coordinator, or what I would describe more accurately, being in everybody's way. She was trying to negotiate with the director to take her business card so he could keep in touch with her if he ever needed any make-up products for the models. My dad couldn't make it because he was volunteering for a career fair that was happening at campus. He promised to make it to the dinner party later that night, though.

Mom and Dad always accompanied us to the gigs we had. One day, I asked my dad why and he said, "I want you to always know that we are in your corner and support everything you do. Well, everything except the illegal stuff."

When Vanessa was finished, she discussed the terms of her contract with the coordinator and signed on the dotted line while we were packing up her things to head home. On the way out the door, I told my mother that I had to go to the mall to pick up an evening gown for the Bailey's dinner party happening later in the evening.

I got into my car and headed to the mall. I had mixed feelings about going to the dinner party. I wanted to go because I just love dinner parties, but I didn't want to go because these were the same people who rejected my photos and chose my *sister*! Do you think I really wanted to celebrate with them?

I went from store to store, but there was just nothing that caught my attention, so I decided to walk into a beauty salon. After two hours, I checked my watch and it was already ten minutes to three. My hair was done, but I still hadn't found a dress. *Time is running out. I need to find a dress!*

I walked down a couple shops from the hair salon and there it was—a potential dress for the evening. It was a tan color with gold shimmers and it hugged the body in all the right places, stopping at the ankles. I went in and asked for a size eight.

The sales woman led me to a rack with about six dresses on it. She pushed through each one checking the tags until she got to a size eight. She handed me the dress and pointed me to a dressing room.

I examined the dress, sweeping it up in my hands en route to the dressing room. I looked up to see where I was going and I saw *him*. "Mark!" I screeched.

He was standing at the entrance of the women's dressing room. He turned around, but not in enough time to see me. I darted behind some racks of dresses before I could be spotted. I watched him look around in wonderment, then begin to browse another area of the store.

When I saw his back, I felt safe enough to make a run for the dressing room. I snatched the number from the sales associate and closed the door behind me. My back was up against the wall and I thought, *Why is he here? I hope he didn't see me. Why don't I want him to see me? Who is he? Wait, why is he in a women's store? Who is he with? Is he with his girlfriend?*

The tan dress with the gold shimmering was no longer my main attraction—Mark was. I didn't care who was looking at me as I crept out of the dressing room and peered around the corner to see where he was and who he was with. I looked and saw him standing by a rack of dresses with some woman and an associate. The associate handed the woman a dress and pointed to the dressing rooms. I darted back into mine. I waited for a while until I thought a comfortable amount of time passed when the woman would have tried her dress on and they would have left. I came out of the room with my dress on to see how I looked in the full size mirror outside of the dressing room. I wanted to see if I could comfortably walk around in this fitted dress. All the while, two associates were staring at me awkwardly, probably because of my game of hide-and-seek with myself. I didn't care though. I just didn't want him to see me.

I was looking at myself, and pleased with my selection, ready to head back to my dressing room when I heard a voice say, "I think that's the one." I saw this happen before, at the studio. Except now he was the one behind me while I was staring at him through the mirror. I turned around and said, "Thank you. It's good to have a second opinion because this is the one I was going to go with."

"Have you been here this whole time?" He asked.

"Wh-why do you ask?"

"Well because I've been in this store for an hour with her and she has tried on like seven dresses and still hasn't made a choice. Since I've been in here this long, I thought that I would have seen you," he said.

"Not necessarily. This store is kind of big, and if you're on one side there is no way that I could see you on the other side."

"No, that can't be, because this store isn't that big, actually." We both took a step out of the dressing room and looked around.

"But it is possible for you not to see me, because when you women shop, ya'll shop." He laughed. "It's Truly, right?"

"Yeah, that's right. You are like the only person who has remembered my name. Usually people call me Tracy or Teresa. But I don't get offended because it's a name you don't hear often."

"What do you do Truly? You dance?"

"Well, I did, a long time ago. I'm thinking about getting back into it. That day I saw you, I was just looking around. Right now I work at a coffeehouse."

"Which one?" He asked.

"You know the one in Midtown where all the shops are?"

"Yeah, I know which one you're talking about. I take my mother down there for lunch sometimes. There's this restaurant nearby she loves."

The conversation was interrupted too soon when a dressing room door opened and a woman stepped out.

"This dress didn't work. So I'll keep my end of the bargain and get this other one so we can go," she said, holding a blue dress up to his face before turning and looking at me.

Mark introduced us. "Miranda, this is Truly; Truly, this is Miranda."

She stuck out her hand and said, "Hello," with the biggest grin on her face.

I returned the gesture, but my grin wasn't so big.

"It was nice seeing you again Truly, but we have to go. We agreed that this was the last dress she would try on. Whether it fits or not, that's it, we're going."

He grabbed her hand as she waved good-bye, then paid for the dress. I watched them walk out of the store, together.

After working the dress off of my body, I got dressed, paid for it, and jumped into my car. It was 4:57 p.m. Just enough time to get home and ready for the dinner party, which started at seven o' clock.

My mother started shouting at about six o' clock for

everyone to wrap it up so we could all head out together. My mother's makeup was on, but her hair was still in rollers. My sister had everything on except for her dress. My dad was the first to be ready, a full hour ago. He was sipping a cup of coffee in the living room and reading. I... well I was almost ready except my hair, which became really frizzy when I had taken a steamy shower when I got home. After getting all the straight pieces flattened with some gel, I met everyone downstairs and we headed off to the party.

The hotel was extravagant. Dad pulled up and we were all greeted with a smile from the valet. He kindly opened my mother's door, and pulled her gently from the car with one hand.

We walked in together, but my mother and father were pulled away quickly by a couple who they knew, but didn't look familiar to me. My sister and I both were looking around at all the fixtures and furniture. I wandered off, just to look around. Everything was fancy. There were waiters and waitresses in tuxedos and white gloves serving caviar and wine. I grabbed a piece of chilled shrimp from a platter a waiter was bringing around the room. There was a huge glass chandelier in the middle of the lobby and under it was a host of people nibbling on fancy food, sipping wine, and listening to sweet, soft music being played by a gentleman on a piano. I was about to walk over to a portrait on the wall, when I heard my mother calling for me to follow my family up the escalator to the room where the dinner and presentations were.

When we arrived at the top of the escalator, there was a grand ballroom. It could fit fifteen-hundred people, easily. We went into the ballroom, where all the lights were out except the little tea light candles on the tables. They lit up the room just enough for one to mingle and find the waiters who were carrying the wine and appetizers.

My mother handed the greeter a card and he replied, "Welcome, Michaels family. Follow me, and I will escort you to your table."

We all smiled, said thank you, and obediently followed the greeter to a table set for five. The centerpiece was a plate of white roses, floating in a plate of water, with the stems cut off and the napkins folded in the shape of a bird. All of us took our seats and just stared awkwardly around until my mom and sister were greeted by the director of the photo campaign.

"Hello Michaels family, so glad to have all of you here. Vanessa, do you mind coming with me to sign the guest book and to pick up your portfolio that Bailey's has prepared for you?"

"Yes, I sure will," she said.

"I'll come with you," my mom said, inviting herself to tag along.

"She's not a baby you know, Mom; take the bottle out of her mouth," I said.

My dad and I both looked at each other and laughed.

"I don't know why Mom is like that," I said to my dad.

"She just is. But she means well. She loves you girls and just wants the best for you two."

*Feels like the best for Vanessa*, I said to myself.

I felt him staring at me as I looked toward the direction of where my mother and sister went.

"How are you, baby? We haven't just sat down and talked in a while. Tell me what's going on?" he asked.

"Nothing much," I told him, with a shrug of my shoulders.

"You look pretty tonight and your hair is beautiful. When you get that done?"

"I went to the mall and I got my hair done and bought this dress today after Vanessa's shoot."

"So what's really going on with you? There has to be more than 'nothing much'," he said, mimicking my shoulder shrug.

"Okay, there is something. I've decided to audition for a performance at the Academy Dance downtown," I told him.

"What? Wow! So you're going to start dancing again and you haven't told me? When did you decide all of this?"

"I don't know. One day I was at work, and I came across the flyer. I feel like it is just something I need to do," I said.

"I am so proud of you. It is my belief that you were born to dance, and you feel like it is something you're supposed to do because you were born to glorify God with dance," he said.

"I haven't told anybody except Casey of course, and now you. I'm just not ready to tell anybody else yet."

"Don't worry pumpkin; your secret's safe with me," he promised.

Dad and I started on some small talk until my mother came back, joining us at the table. She had this enormous grin on her face, reminding me of the joker from those Batman movies. I thought, *What is she up to now?*

Dad asked my Mom, "Pamela, what are you up to now?"

She was really fidgety, obviously having information that we didn't know, but wanted.

"There is this guy named Terrell. He's—" She didn't finish before my dad interrupted, "He's Bill and Clarissa's boy."

"Yes!" She said, excited that she and Dad were on the same page.

"And so what about him?" he asked, confused.

"I bumped into Clarissa on my way back to the table and we started talking. I found out that she is here with her son Terrell, who is also a model for Bailey's. See, they already have something in common," she explained.

"So she told me that he was looking to settle down

and she has been talking to him about Vanessa. See he's over there talking to that man by the stage, with the glasses on. Do you see them?"

My Dad and I stretched our necks to see who this Terrell person was until she said, "Oh my goodness, here he comes."

Terrell was tall, dark, and handsome; you know the saying.

"Hello Mrs. Michaels, Mr. Michaels. And this must be the beautiful Vanessa," he said, grabbing my hand and kissing it.

My mother jumped up, grabbing my hand from his embrace, "No, no, no. This is our youngest daughter, Truly. Vanessa is on the other side of the ballroom right now."

Terrell responded, never taking his eyes off of me, "Well, that's unfortunate."

The moment was very awkward, as now every person at the table was staring at me. My dad interrupted the awkwardness by stretching out his hand, "I'm Brian. So you are a model for Bailey's?"

"Yes, I am and have been for about five years."

"I find it interesting that you and Vanessa haven't met," my dad noted.

"Well, there is no real relationship with the other models unless I am doing an ad campaign with them. Other than that, we all have our own photo shoot times and really don't cross paths," Terrell explained.

"Alright, well that makes sense," Dad said.

"I wish I could stay and talk, but I better get back to the guest I came with. It was nice meeting you all. Hopefully I can meet Vanessa really soon."

We all nodded our heads in agreement and watched him walk away until he found another conversation to enter into.

"That was really weird," I said to break the silence.

"It was. Well, I'm not going to tell her about him to-night." Mom said. "I want her to focus on herself. They can meet later."

I decided to excuse myself to the restroom because the cocktails started to get to me. I searched and searched until finally I asked one of the bartenders where the ladies room was. I was freshening up when I saw Vanessa come out of one of the stalls, "Hey girl, I haven't seen you all night. You enjoying yourself?" I asked.

"Yes, I am. Everything is good. Everybody is so nice. They've been, like, waiting on me hand and foot. This was just a photo shoot. I can only imagine what happens when a person actually becomes famous," she said. "What about you? I mean you've been stuck with Mom and Dad all night," she laughed.

"Dad is cool as you know, but Mom on the other hand…"

"I know, you don't even have to tell me."

"She's been playing matchmaker."

"What do you mean?" she asked me, taking some pink

lipstick from her purse.

I stared at her while she applied it to her lips. My sister *was* very beautiful, I couldn't argue about that. Her skin was really fair. She could pull off those bright colors like pink, orange, and yellow. The pink of the dress she had on was soft and slim-fit. I could tell that she and my mom took some time finding that one. Her hair was pinned up with a bun in the front—what I will call a modern version of the pin up. Since she was modeling, she now had access to those celebrity hairstylists. My Mom and sister seemed to always be close, ever since we were younger. Even though I loved to dance, I really wasn't a girly girl. I loved hanging with Dad. My sister and mother always went shopping, tried different types of makeup, and read those silly, gossip magazines.

"Truly, what do you mean?" she asked again.

"Oh. She's gonna try and hook you up with some guy named Terrell, whose Momma's name is Clarissa."

Her body slowly lifted as we stared at each other through the mirror, "Good. I need a man. I'm ready to get out of that house!" she said.

I thought, *That's not the answer I was expecting but more power to ya.*

"You're not supposed to know this information I just told you. So act surprised when Momma introduces you to him."

"Why wouldn't she want me to know?" Vanessa asked.

"She doesn't want you to be distracted from what you're doing tonight. Business first, love second."

We both nodded at each other. If my sister and I didn't have anything else in common, we did share the same mother.

"Is he cute?" she asked.

"He's cool. But I don't know what you like; you'll have to be the judge of that."

The rest of the night turned out pretty nicely. Dinner was amazing, and I was proud to see my sister in the ad for Bailey's. It was good to see something successful coming from all of those years of hard work.

The dance auditions were just six days away. I was determined to stick to my plan to start preparing a routine for Saturday's audition, but we got home so late last night from the dinner party that all I had energy to do was put on my pajamas and go to sleep. After coming home from Sunday morning church service, I thought today would be the perfect day to begin. I asked my dad where he kept all the old videos that he had recorded of my dance recitals when I was younger. He showed me where he had them boxed up in the den and brought out an old dusty VCR and hooked it up to the TV in my bedroom. I popped in a tape that read, "First dance recital. Fall 1990."

I saw myself, a dozen other little girls, and a few boys teeter-totter around a stage in white leotards and pink tutus. I laughed as I finally identified myself on the tape.

I didn't realize how much I missed dancing until then. For a couple of hours, I put in more videos and watched dance recitals of myself as I got older—stumbling less, becoming more graceful. I fumbled through the box and found a tape that read, "First solo performance, Spring 2000," and popped it in the VCR.

I fast forwarded past my mother saying something into the camera while my sister held up "bunny ears" behind her head. I went a little too far, so I had to rewind. I watched myself confidently dancing the choreographed routine. I executed leaps and arabesque positions, balancing on one leg and bending forward while standing as straight and strong as possible on the other. I was so proud of myself, and happy that I did have something that I could call my own. No one could take this gift from me, not even my sister. I continued watching and everything I had ever known about ballet dancing started flowing out of me. I started calling, by name, each move that I executed. I grabbed a piece of paper and wrote down exactly what I was doing on the tape. All of a sudden I heard the door bell ring... and ring... and ring. I tried to ignore it until I realized no one else was going to answer it.

I jumped up and ran downstairs. There was no one in sight. I heard my mother yelling from upstairs for my dad to get the door. I walked past the dining room and the table was set for four. It was set with tea cups; tea-cake and china Mom only pulls out on special occasions.

I began to wonder who was on the other side of this door. I opened it and there was Terrell.

"Hel-lo a-gain, Truly," he said.

*Is he here for me or for Vanessa?* I thought.

Mom came behind me, "Don't be rude Truly, let the gentleman in."

I stepped back as he came in and hugged my mother. Dad came shortly and they greeted with a firm hand-shake. My mother informed Terrell that Vanessa would be down shortly.

"Truly, go get that pot of tea off of the fire for me," my mom asked, while she escorted Terrell and Dad into the dining room.

"I'll help," Terrell said.

I could feel my mother glaring at me, so I said, "No that's okay, I got it. You're a guest so just sit down and relax." I guess that was the correct answer because she relaxed and took her seat.

I came in with the pot of tea and placed it in the center of the table. Terrell asked me, "So Truly, what school do you attend?"

"I'm actually not in college right now. I didn't take that route. I work at a coffee shop."

"I mean, then, what do you do? What do you like? There has to be something that you love to do besides pour cups of coffee," Terrell said.

"There actually is…I like to dance."

"Here she is finally, Vanessa, the daughter you came

to meet." My mother interrupted as she grabbed Vanessa by the arm and pointed to the seat that was across from Terrell's.

"Thank you so much Truly, but you can go now," my mother said.

"It was a pleasure seeing you again Truly, it really was," Terrell said, smiling.

I went upstairs and saw that the video had played to the end because the screen had static all over it. I picked up the note pad that I had been writing on and decided that I was going to go over to Casey's and prepare for the audition.

Casey was at work, so she gave me her house key and told me to just go and practice. She said she would meet me at her house after she got off of work. I arrived at her house and began immediately putting a plan together for a great solo performance. I was confident that I would be chosen to perform the *pas de deux*, because like my dad said, "I was born to dance."

When Casey arrived home at about 12:30 a.m., I was still practicing. She handed me a single rose with a card on it.

"What's this?" I asked her.

"Why don't you tell me? The delivery guy brought it to the shop for you today."

"Someone delivered only one rose?" I asked.

"I know, right." Casey said, "So you tell me what guy you got whipped?"

"A guy whipped? I don't have a guy whipped. If I had an interest you would know about him," I told her.

I opened the little card that was attached to the flower. It said, "Just thinking about you."

Casey walked from behind me and plopped on her couch, "If that's what you get when he's thinking about you, I would like to see what he would do for you when you're actually together."

We didn't talk for much longer because she kicked me out, saying that I had too much energy for her to keep up with. I did! I was so excited about the auditions. I had a new secret admirer. This was the most excitement I'd had in a long time—since I won the "Best Drink Mixer" contest at work, actually.

I put my dance roughly together. I decided to use the rest of the week perfecting it. I got home about 2:00 a.m., pulling into my parking space behind my mother's car. I crept into the house as quietly as possible. Feeling my way around the kitchen, I flicked the light on. I stuck my head into the fridge to see if I had any apple juice left, when my mother startled me.

"Truly," she said.

"Momma you scared the mess out of me. I'm sorry if I woke you up. I tried to be as quiet as possible," I said.

"What do you think you are doing?" She asked me.

"Getting a drink before I go to bed."

"I saw the way you were trying to flirt with Terrell today," she said.

"What!" I hissed. "What? That is not true; what are you talking about?"

"You were pretty much all over him. Heck, if I wasn't there you would have tried to take him for yourself," she said.

I was standing there with no real defense, frozen like a person with a loose dog charging at them.

"You know what? You have always been jealous of your sister. But I'm not going to let you take this from her, and definitely not from me."

My mother slammed the fridge door and walked out.

I was confused, and more hurt than words could express. I grabbed my bag and went to my room.

The next day my mom and I didn't talk to each other. At dinner, she was a lot quieter than usual and even more so and distant whenever I had something to say. I tried to avoid going to dinner that day, but Dad said he wanted all of us to eat together when we were all home so that he could spend time with us. I don't think he knew what happened between my mother and me. After dinner I went straight up stairs, showered, and headed for bed. Although I wanted to care that my mother was giving me the silent treatment, my mind was too occupied with the steps of my future routine. I lay in bed dozing off and on. My desire to start practicing for the *pas de deux* was so strong. I couldn't wait to fall asleep in anticipation of tomorrow at the same time I didn't want to let the dancing me in my head rest. There was a game of tug-of-war going on in my brain until the desire to release this day to the past won; I gave into sleep. My goal was to rise before the sun to start practicing.

I got up in the morning later than I would have liked, but I was pleased with the work I did on my routine before going into work.

I returned home for the evening completely exhausted, I tossed my bag down, joining my Dad in the living room where he was watching TV.

"No dinner tonight?" I asked, kissing him on the cheek.

"Nope, your sister has a date tonight. I've already eaten but you can order take-out."

"Are you paying?" I asked. He didn't reply.

"Daddy?"

"Yes, yes whatever you want just take it," he said without looking away from the tube.

"That's how you always get'em," I said to myself walking upstairs to my room.

I passed the bathroom and Vanessa was fogging it up with a can of hair spray.

"A date on a Tuesday?" I asked her.

"Terrell has a shoot out of town this weekend. So we're hooking up tonight."

"Where's Mom?" I asked.

"She's at Clarissa's house. They planned a makeup party. Clarissa knows a bunch of women, so Mom is shopping around for some new clients."

"They kick'n it, huh?" I asked.

"I guess."

I stood there a second before asking, "How do you feel about Terrell?"

"He's cool. I don't have any deep feelings; we just met Sunday."

"How do you think I feel about him?"

"I don't know Truly, what am I supposed to think?" she asked, confusedly.

"So you aren't having any crazy thoughts about me and Terrell, are you?"

"Noooo," she said.

"Good. Well, have fun tonight."

I went back downstairs to take Dad up on his offer for take-out. I was feeling Chinese. I sat on the couch watching TV with my Dad while devouring some beef and broccoli lo mein when the doorbell rang. I knew exactly who it was, and I was not about to get it. Vanessa came rushing down the stairs. Terrell came in and my father got up to greet him. Then Terrell greeted me, but I left the response short and sweet with very little eye contact.

Dad and I watched movies for the rest of the night. I looked at the clock on the cable box which read, 11:10 p.m. I looked around. I had outlasted my Dad; he was in his chair snoring. The front door opened and it was Mom. She chuckled when she saw Dad asleep in his chair.

"Now, he knows he has to go to work in the morning. You should have sent him to bed," she told me.

Happy she was acknowledging my presence, I said, "I can't make Dad go to bed."

She smiled while she helped him up to bed, ignoring his groaning and moaning to stay in his comfy chair.

I then followed, retiring to my room.

Wednesday morning, I was awake in bed thinking about my life. I was thinking about the audition. I was thinking about Academy Dance. I was thinking about Mark. I was thinking about the rose. *Who could be my secret admirer?* All kinds of thoughts were running through my mind. *I have to make something happen in the next two years of my life. I am ready for the auditions. I wonder how long Mark has been dating Miranda.*

Since I took the entire week off to prepare for the auditions, I decided I wasn't going to hang around the house all day. So I went to visit Lily.

I got there and there was a class in session. Lily stuck her head out of her office and invited me in. On the way back, there were little girls as young as six years old learning to dance ballet. A rush of satisfaction filled my heart as I watched them giggle at each other when they tumbled over after trying to balance on one leg.

I reached Lily's office and she asked, "Is there anything I can do for you today?"

"No, I was just coming by to see you. I had such a

great time last time I was here and you were so nice to me. I thought it rude for me to never come back and see how you are," I said.

"How kind of you," she said with a smile. "Since you ask how I am, I am great, as long as I can see those little faces in there," she said, pointing out the door. I knew exactly who she was talking about. "Unfortunately, I can't do this forever," her smile turning solemn.

"Why not? Isn't this what you love?" I asked.

"Yes, but I feel I'm being called away from this place. I feel that this place is going in a different direction. You know, kind of like a Moses and Joshua type thing? I'm just not yet sure who's Joshua." she said. "Anywho. I know you haven't come here to be bothered with my mess."

"No, I like talking with you Lily. I really do."

"So why not come to lunch with me? Do you have time?"

"I sure do," I said.

Lily and I walked to her favorite Greek restaurant a couple of shops down from the studio. Lunch was great. We talked like we'd known each other longer than a couple of weeks.

As a matter of fact, the entire day was great, as I spent the rest of it with Lily. Spending time with her was like spending time with a second mother. I have not had a connection like that with anyone other than my dad in a long time. I didn't leave Academy Dance until an hour after it was closed. I didn't get to see Mark, but hanging with Lily was just as cool.

I pulled up to my house around 8:00 p.m. Everyone's cars were parked in the driveway and all the lights were on downstairs. I figured they were eating dinner or cleaning up. Either way, I was starving. I opened the door, but neither one of my expectations were correct. I was way off. Something bad had happened and I knew I had something to do with it when I saw my mother's eyes.

# Three

I stood before my family as I watched Vanessa sitting on the couch bawling into my dad's shoulder. My mother was sitting on the other couch staring at me. Vanessa looked at me, got up, and left the room. My mother silently followed her. I stood there until my father said, "What's going on Truly?"

"Dad, as you can see I just walked through the door. I have no idea," I said.

"So you really don't know why your sister's angry?" He asked me seriously, more serious than I have seen him in a long time. It kind of frightened me.

"Terrell told her today that he couldn't see her any longer. That it just wouldn't work out because he had feelings for you. And if he couldn't date you than he really didn't want to have anything to do with this family."

I was shocked, confused, and defensive all at the same time, "So what does that have to do with me, Dad?"

"How this has to do with you is that your mother said that she saw you flirting with Terrell when he came over on Sunday."

"That's not true, that's cra—"

"And Vanessa," he interrupted, "said that you asked her yesterday how she felt about Terrell, maybe implying that you may have some interest in him."

"I only asked her that because Mom came and confronted me Sunday night, saying that I wanted him and that I was flirting with him and stuff. But none of that is true. I asked Vanessa that to see if she felt the same way."

I had barely finished talking when my mother came busting down the stairs, "I knew it! I knew it! You thought that you were going to be slick and try to take him from her. But he ended up giving into your seduction!"

"My seduction! You're crazy! You better get out of my face talking that mess," I shouted.

"Do not talk to your mother like that. You apologize right now!" Dad yelled.

I can't remember the last time my dad had been angry with me. I was hurt. My mother convinced him that I am a bad person. Why? Why is there so much animosity between my mother and me?

I apologized, walked up to my room, grabbed a week's worth of clothes, and stormed out the door. On the way out, I heard my dad ask me where I was going, but I didn't respond. I could hear my mother telling him to let me go.

I went to the coffeehouse so that I could ask Casey if I could stay with her until things calmed down at home. She offered me the keys to her apartment, but I didn't want to be alone. So, she made another offer to me: a warm vanilla latte. The cup of coffee didn't erase what just happened, but it sure helped. I sat down in a chair facing the window. I held the cup of coffee to my lips without even taking a sip, thinking, *I can't believe this just happened.* Suddenly, I heard a voice behind me say, "Can I sit here?" I looked up. It was Mark.

"Yeah, sure, sit down." I said softly.

"I was just stopping by to get a coffee and I saw you sitting here. I thought it was you but wasn't sure. I remembered seeing you with that ring on at the mall."

I looked at my hand. "Why would you know what kind of ring I am wearing?" I asked, a little too harshly.

"Whoa, is something wrong? I didn't mean to offend you. I'm sorry for coming over here. I'll just leave."

He started to walk away when I stopped him, "That's not necessary. I am having a bad evening but that is in no way your fault, so I apologize." He took his seat.

"Are you all right? Can I help?" Mark asked.

"No. I really don't feel like talking about it right now. Thanks for the offer."

"Okay." He relaxed back into his chair, taking a sip of his coffee, slowly.

"So where's Miranda?" I asked, not really interested in where she was but for the sake of bringing her up.

He sat up to answer my question. "I'm not sure. I don't really keep up with her," he said.

"Why not? You're going to see her later."

"I hope you don't get offended, but I think it's a little

weird that you are asking me where my cousin is like she's my girl—" he stopped. "You thought that Miranda was my girlfriend, didn't you?"

Relieved and embarrassed—but more relieved—I said, "I mean, I saw ya'll together."

"So she has to be my girlfriend because we were at the mall? Miranda is my cousin who dances at the Academy Dance. She was getting a dress for an award she was receiving that night. She asked me to give her a ride to the mall. That's all. I don't even have a girlfriend."

"I am so sorry. I apologize for jumping to conclusions."

"Forgiven," he said.

We sat in silence for a brief moment until he asked, "So what's going on, if you don't mind me asking?"

"So, you *are* going to make me talk about it," I laughed.

"I'm interested. I want to know what or who would want to make you upset."

*Wow,* I thought. But for some reason I still couldn't bring myself to tell him what was going on.

I wanted to say, "My parents just accused me of trying to take a man from my sister who wasn't hers to begin with and I refuse to keep letting my mother treat me like crap." Instead, I said, "I work here. Sometimes I come just to have a cup of coffee after a long day."

Mark started shaking his head, "No, no, no. Not me. I couldn't come to my job to relax. I would never go to my job unless I was working," he said.

"That's not true. You've been at Academy Dance even when you're not working," I argued.

"Naw, that doesn't count. That place is like home. Plus, Academy Dance is not my job. I dance because I love to. I've grown up around dance all of my life. My parents danced in college, where they met. My dad danced until he had his accident."

I started having an out of body experience. I couldn't believe that the guy I had a serious crush on was sitting with me, did not have a girlfriend, and was having coffee on what seemed to be the worst day of my life.

"He is now paralyzed from the waist down. I dance for him. I dance for all my loved ones, those who can't dance for themselves. That's why I have stuck to it this long. I do it for passion. As for my job, I am an accountant. I work from home so that I can have the free time to dance whenever and take care of my daughter."

I choked on the coffee that was trying to go down my throat. "Y-you have a daughter?"

"Yes, and she is my everything," he said with a big smile.

We sat quietly. It was the best silence that I have ever enjoyed. I didn't realize that I liked him so much, or why I did. There was just this unexplainable connection that I felt between the two of us.

"I have to go. Sorry I didn't get to find out more about you, but I was supposed to have already gotten my daughter from my parents. It was very nice to see you. Maybe I'll see you again."

"Yeah, sure, and have a good evening," I said.

As soon as he was out of site, Casey ran and jumped in my lap, "Girl who was that cute guy talking to you?"

"That's Mark. He happens to be the son of the director of Academy Dance. You know the place where we are going this Saturday for my auditions?"

"Yes, which I took the day off for," she said.

"He's cute but he has a daughter. I don't know about that."

"What's wrong with that?" Casey asked.

"Well I just don't want to be mixed up with no crazy, you know what I mean?"

"Yeah, I know what you mean," she agreed.

I helped her close down the shop by straightening up the lobby while she took care of "behind the counter" duties. Soon we were at her place, and I was explaining to her what happened hours ago with my family. She let me know that I could stay with her as long as I needed to. She threw me a blanket, and I fell asleep on her sofa.

Thursday morning I woke with a slight headache, but I was determined to make the day a productive one. I saw that my phone had a missed call and a voice message. I listened to it. The message was Dad telling me to come to the house at 7:00 p.m. so that we could talk about the previous night over dinner.

It was only two days before the competition. I couldn't waste any more time. I had to use each day to perfect my dance for the audition. Once my body was ready, I practiced for hours, putting all my frustration, anger, and hopes for the future into this dance.

As I danced, Casey's question, "Who are you?" kept playing over in my mind. With every *balancé, devant* and extention I asked myself, "Who am I?"

Speaking out loud, "I dance because I'm born to. I dance because I'm happy when I do it. I dance because…" I paused. "Then why has it taken me so long to just dance?"

I reached the point where I felt I did all the dancing I could do for the day. I looked at my cell; it was a little after 3:00 p.m. I grabbed a drink of water, plopped down onto the sofa, my temporary bed. "Why am I so invested in this dance? What will it matter anyway?"

I sat with my eyes closed; a peace came over me. I meditated. *Go… do… try, even if you don't know what is going to happen.*

"You are a dancer," said a small, still response.

I immediately jumped up with excitement. Throwing my arms into the air, "I know who I am! I know what my gift is! That's it! I am a dancer! I am a ballerina! One day, I'm gonna amaze people with my beautiful dancing. One day, I'm gonna have my own company!" I shouted.

I strutted around the house singing what felt like a new song. I freshened up and ate some lunch. I had a few hours to go before I joined my family for dinner.

After cleaning up my dishes, I decided to do my Bible study and prayer before going to my parents. I grabbed my Bible out of my duffle bag. I wasn't sure what I wanted to study. I flipped through the pages until I noticed some notes I had written in the back of the book, "Oh I remember these notes from a Sunday service. Looks like these notes are from a couple of months ago," I said to myself.

I wrote, *Don't worry about your life. God doesn't create anything without purpose. Nothing that leaves the mouth of God returns to Him void (Isaiah 55:11). Seek God and He will direct your path.*

My eyes scanned over my scribbling on the page.

Jeremiah 29:11 was written in the right-hand corner of the page. I immediately flipped to the book of Jeremiah, the 29th chapter. I took my finger and followed the small numbers until I located verse 11. It read, *"For I know the plans I have for you," says the Lord. "They are plans for good and not for disaster, to give you a future and a hope."*

The peace I felt before was present over me again. I stared at the verse for what seemed like hours rejoicing over the fact that I was not a mistake. Even though I didn't know what tomorrow held, God knows because He created me.

I concluded my Bible study with prayer. I closed my eyes, praying with my heart, "God, I am going to stop aimlessly living my life. I am going to live for You. I am going to seek You for direction. I am going to put You first by doing what you want me to do. I do have purpose."

I prayed for my family, I thanked God for His goodness, for the gift of dance He has given me and for the opportunity to audition for the *pas de deux*.

I had about three hours until dinner over at my parent's, so I laid down to rest.

I headed to the house around 6:30 p.m., not really knowing what to expect when I got there. I came in but the only two who were in the kitchen were Dad and Vanessa. I silently went to the sink to wash my hands. Dad came over and gave me a hug then said, "Vanessa."

"Hello, Truly," my sister forced herself to say.

We all sat down at the table and started passing dinner around. "You're mother couldn't be here. She obligated herself to a makeup party for a bridal shower. She wanted to cancel but I wouldn't let her. So here we are."

My sister and I both continued eating in silence.

My Dad took a couple of bites of his macaroni and cheese and then asked if we had anything we wanted to say. Vanessa spoke first, "You know, Dad. You and Mom were right to give Truly her name, because just like her name, she is very unpopular. I mean really, how many Truly's have you heard of?"

"Vanessa, this dinner is to bring peace. You're not helping by saying that," Dad said.

"Did you know, Dad, that Vanessa 'The Witch' Michaels would have been a more suitable name for her. Don't you think?"

"All right girls, enough! This clearly is not working."

"I don't even know why you invited me here!" I shouted.

"Because I wanted us to discuss this."

"You wanted to discuss what? Huh. You had already made your mind up yesterday who you believed. So stop this fake act like you just want us to be a family. No, you just don't want to stand up to Momma cause you have to share the rest of your life with her. I'm out of here."

"Watch it, Truly. You may be grown, but you do not talk to me like that."

"No, Dad, you watch this." I grabbed my purse and slammed the front door. I went back to Casey's apartment, which I decided was going to be my new home.

It was Friday. The audition was tomorrow. I only practiced my routine one time in front of Casey, who approved it with hand claps and cheers. I wanted to relax today and focus on my relationship with God. Besides Casey, I felt like He was all I had. I made sure in my prayers to thank Jesus for blessing me with Casey as a friend. Even though I had this great blessing of a friend in my life, my relationship with my family was crumbling around me. My dad called me throughout the day, but I didn't answer. He left messages to let me know when I was ready to deal with this, then I was welcome to come back home. My father apologized for not waiting for my mother before inviting me over to handle the problem. He thought that it would have gone better if she were there. He also apologized for Vanessa's behavior. It was his guess that it was too early for her to deal with the issue. I listened to the messages but was wondering why my dad was the only one dishing out all of the apologies. I had no intentions of calling him back, for now. They weren't ready to be confronted with the way I felt about everyone attacking me, as if I were the enemy and not a part of their family. I definitely was going to handle this issue when I was ready, and now was not the time. The only important thing to me was Saturday.

I spent all of Friday and most of Saturday by myself. Casey went to her parent's house on Friday night for her older sister's birthday celebration. She decided to spend the night there since it finished so late, but promised she wouldn't miss the audition for anything. I rested until I woke up around 7:00 a.m. Saturday morning. I prayed, practiced, and waited for Casey to arrive so that we could go to the audition together. We left from her apartment around 4:30 p.m., heading for Academy Dance.

We arrived a little before 5:00 p.m. The place was swarming with people trying to get registered for the auditions for the Fall performance. But it was double the women dancers who were trying out for the *pas de deux*.

Since we were an hour ahead of the start time, there was no rush to get in. We parked her car in the nearest parking space. I chose to take my time making my way to the registration table to get my number because everyone else was rushing around and looking very nervous. I decided that I would take it easy by taking my time. Casey and I got into a line to get to a lady who was handing out clipboards. "Who needs a clipboard? Raise your hand and we will get one to you."

Casey raised her hand. The lady came back with a clipboard. It was Miranda.

"I've met you before, at the mall. What's your name again?" she asked me.

"Truly," I said.

"Truly, that's right. I did not know you were a dancer. That's how you knew my cousin, Mark."

"I met Mark here. I never knew him before here, nor have I danced in this town before."

"So what are you auditioning for?"

"The *pas de deux*," I said.

"Oh, the solo with Mark. Okay, well, good luck." She smiled and kept searching for hands that were raised.

*The solo is with Mark? This cannot be happening, this cannot be happening to me,* I thought. I covered my face with my hands, now *feeling* as nervous as everyone else *looked*.

"Oh no! So, you just saw who I saw?" Casey said.

"No, what do you mean?"

"You covered your face so I thought you saw her, too."

"Saw who, Casey?" I said anxiously.

"Vanessa."

# Four

I never thought a day would come that I would cringe at the sight of seeing one of my family members in public. The way I felt seeing Vanessa handing her clipboard to the registration desk, trading it for a number, was the way I felt when I saw an ex-boyfriend in public. I was dodging her.

"What the heck is she doing here?" Casey asked. "I'm about to go find out."

"No girl. You cannot start any mess up in here. You're with me and we can't get kicked out or I'll look bad."

"You're right. I'll just handle her two-timing self after the auditions."

We finally made our way to the registration table and got my number. We walked into the dance room and people were stretching and getting pumped up by loved ones they brought with them. I looked around the room, and I saw my mother going out of the room carrying some of Vanessa's things. I was pulling things out of my bag to pin down my hair when Vanessa came over.

"Need some help getting ready, sister?" she asked.

"What do you want? How did you know about this place?"

"Mom told me about it weeks ago. She found a piece of paper while she was doing the laundry. I've been preparing since then. So why didn't you tell me li'l sis? Hmmm? You still wanted to keep your little ballet slippers a secret?" she taunted, pushing a piece of hair into place that didn't get caught with the rest of my hair.

"I'll ask you again, what do you want?"

"I figured since you thought that you would bring some competition to my love life, why be mad at you? I'll just return the favor."

"You're not even ready for the audition."

"Me, not ready? For what audition? The *pas de deux*? I was ready weeks ago. I started getting ready when Mom told me. I wasn't sure if I wanted to do it, but you gave me no choice."

I couldn't believe what I was hearing. I turned away from Vanessa in attempt to ignore her.

People's family members started clearing the room as Mark requested them to.

Casey walked up to us, "Hey, that's the guy that was feeling you at the coffeehouse... Oh, hi Vanessa."

"Oh, is he?" Vanessa said devilishly.

Mark looked very busy instructing people who had questions for him. I nervously made eye contact with him and he started heading my way, "No, not now," I said.

"Truly, what are you doing here? You didn't tell me you were trying out. What position?"

"Surprise, the solo position," I said.

Vanessa butted in, "I'm Vanessa by the way. And you

are…"

"Mark. Nice to meet you."

"Mark," I said. "This is Casey, my friend. She works at the coffeehouse as well."

"I know. Casey makes a good cappuccino without all the fluffy syrups. Real coffee," he noted.

She proudly gave us a smile.

"I have to go and get ready to judge the performances. I wish you both the best," he said, before turning away to another band of people with questions.

"So he's your eye candy, huh?" Vanessa said, now in my personal space. "We're just going to see how good this one tastes."

Vanessa left me standing there feeling like crap. Nothing can be lower than that.

The last thirty minutes before auditions started were a blur. My sister and my mother being there was a complete distraction, especially since my mother never came to wish me good luck.

The first auditions were group-style. A large group of people danced on the stage at once and the three judges, Mark, Lily, and another woman named Cecilia Lagoon, watched. The group started with around thirty dancers, dwindling down to about twenty-two, and then fifteen as the judges watched carefully each movement of each dancer. The ones they didn't like, they thanked for auditioning and piled their photos into a separate stack.

The ones who they weren't sure about they asked to

do particular moves. If the dancer executed the move to their liking, they were asked to stay.

I was sitting there more nervous than ever. I didn't know that the other dancer of the *pas de deux* was Mark. And I really didn't know that he was going to be the judge of my audition. The room started clearing as the group performers got their acceptance to the dance team. The atmosphere changed as all the females auditioning for this dance started stretching. Miranda stood up in front of the room.

"As you where informed at the registration table, how this is going to work is you will be called in order by the number that you received as you arrived and registered. Please, as you come forward make sure to hand your number to the judges before you begin. We will announce the dancer who has been chosen at the end of this audition. Good luck. Can number one please come forward to start things out."

I watched as number one danced very gracefully to music that she said was created by her brother specifically for this night. Her performance wasn't that bad, but it wasn't her I worried about. Nor was it any of the others that made me nervous. It was, "Number four, Vanessa."

Even though Vanessa and I both have a background in dance, I felt like she had the advantage over me because she danced all throughout high school. I was, just like Casey said, "Pulling out the old ballet shoes." The ballet shoes that are dusty and old. Maybe Dad was wrong, I wasn't born to dance. Maybe I was wrong, I wasn't a ballerina nor was I going to have my own company. I was born to be the little sister to Vanessa; to just be her shadow.

Vanessa began to dance, and man, she really danced. When she was finished all three judges stood to their feet, applauding her performance. I watched her walk from the stage, hugging our mother.

A few more dancers were before me, and then I heard, "Number eight, Truly." It was now my turn.

I handed my music to the DJ. I took a step to the center of the floor. I felt Mark looking directly at me, but I couldn't make eye contact with him. I looked straight over his head to the onlookers. My music began, and I danced.

# Five

Casey's sofa has been my bed since I left the auditions Saturday night. I didn't get up to go to church today. I didn't do anything. I just laid on the sofa thinking, sleeping, and thinking some more. I cried all night yesterday about being Vanessa's understudy. Nothing Casey said could take away the anger I felt when they announced her as the one who would dance with Mark for the winter charity event in December. Mixed emotions ran through my mind. I felt like there was something that I did that I was being punished for. There was something that God just hadn't forgiven me for. I repented for my sins, but I guess whatever I did just wasn't forgivable, and the punishment for my fault is living in complete darkness to the world. Watching my mother walk out of that place with Vanessa was crushing. But that didn't make me angry. What made me angry was that I thought for once I could win. That's the depressing part. Where did I go wrong? When did Mom and I go wrong? She hates me.

I remember when I was just a girl. It always seemed that I was much closer to my dad than I was to my mother. I remember having memories of him and I doing special things, but none with my Mom. It was my dad who introduced me to dance. I recall dancing as young as four, but it was around six that I can really replay the memories in my mind. Dad was the one who bought me my first pair of pink ballet shoes. I'll never forget the day. He called me into the room, hiding a white shoe box behind his back. He told me to close my eyes. When I opened them there were the shoes, dangling in front of my face.

He said, "Now that I know dancing is what you want to do, here is your first pair of ballet shoes."

I took the shoes from his hand. "But I have shoes already."

"These shoes are special. These are the first shoes you are choosing to wear my dear. A big difference."

I replayed in my mind what Dad said, "These shoes are special. These are your *first* shoes you are *choosing* to wear."

All of a sudden, I had an epiphany. I sat up on the couch shouting to myself, "I know what he meant. What he meant was that dance is who I am because I choose to dance. No one can take that from me. Not Vanessa, not Mom, nobody."

Casey came out of the bathroom brushing her teeth, "Girl, what are you in here shouting about?"

"You're just now brushing your teeth?" I asked.

"No, you didn't. You're not the only one around here who can sleep in. At least I'm brushing my teeth," she said, fussing her way back into the bathroom. "You haven't even brushed yours yet," she continued shouting from the bathroom.

"I've decided that I am going to stick it out," I shouted back. "I am not going to quit. I am going to be Vanessa's understudy. I'm gonna rock it out. I'm gonna hit every practice hard, as if I were the leading lady."

"So you were thinking about quitting?" Casey asked, coming back into the living room.

"Yep, but not now."

"Okay, so since you are feeling better, let's go to the mall to get some fresh air.

Casey was right, I needed to get some fresh air but it didn't seem to help much. After leaving the mall we stopped at my favorite restaurant for dinner. I watched Casey's lips move—my body present, my mind absent. I stared at Casey as she spoke but my mind pondered over and over again the frustration of being my sister's understudy. It wasn't as easy as I thought to just let things be. We got home and I immediately plopped on the couch to sleep. I've had enough for one day.

It's been four days since the audition and about one week since I moved in with Casey. I have been avoiding my family; only doing the minimum: I show up for work and go back to Casey's. I think I'm depressed.

I woke up the next morning rubbing two places: my lower back and my temple. I was rubbing my lower back from sleeping on the couch for a week now, the pain in my lower back was bearing witness to that.

I was rubbing my temple because I just woke up from

having a dream. I've been having these mysterious dreams for one month now. In these reoccurring dreams I have seen myself dancing before a crowd of people. The auditorium is very dim as I see myself take on this unknown solo project. After waking, I've always wondered why am I dancing, and where? Usually, the Giver of dreams only allows me to see myself dancing a beautiful solo. But this time He let me see a little bit more; in my dream I lifted my head and a man's hand was extended to me. I took a hold of his hand before waking up.

I looked around, grabbing my phone, which said 9:46 a.m., I got dressed to head off to work. I didn't have to be there until 1:00 p.m. but I decided to go in early. I grabbed one of my favorite iced drinks and took a seat by the window until my shift started. While I was waiting, I listened to the voicemails that I had been ignoring for the last few days. One of the three messages was from Casey telling me not to wait up for her since she was staying at school late to work on a group art project that was due soon. The second message was from a computer telling me to call this random number to take advantage of their special before it ended.

The third and final message was from my Dad. He said he was calling to say, "Hello" and to see what time we could meet up for lunch. I decided that his message would be the one I responded to.

It was good to talk to my Dad. I talked to him until I

clocked in. No matter what we were going through I could still talk to him as if nothing was wrong.

After getting home from work I showered and laid down for bed. My Dad made me feel comfortable to meet with him for breakfast tomorrow. I couldn't make it for lunch because I had to work. I couldn't wait to see him, catch up, and eat my favorite thing for breakfast—strawberry-covered waffles.

*My hair was short and curly. I had a cracker in my hand, one shoe on, and one shoe off. My Dad had a bag in one hand and me on his hip. He placed me into a car seat in the back of a car. My mother was standing in the doorway of a house with my sister standing next to her.* This is the scene I saw before I woke up. My dreams shifted from dancing a solo to my childhood. It was really weird, so I decided to share my dreams with my Dad when we got together that morning.

I arrived at the Breakfast Nook to meet my father. I stopped at the host's station and asked for him. The host informed me that my father mentioned to him that I was coming, grabbed a menu, and escorted me into the restaurant. There sat my father, mother, and Vanessa. I went through ten different emotions in the matter of seconds; the main one being betrayal.

My father stood as the host brought me to the table. He pulled my seat out and tipped the host before he walked away. I was sitting there feeling really awkward until my mother said, "Hello, Truly. How are you doing this morning?" She asked while touching my hand.

"I'm doing fine, thank you."

I looked at Vanessa next, to see what type of mood she was in. She looked at me with the biggest grin, "Hi, Truly. You must have just got that skirt. It's really cute."

"Thank you, I did."

"None of us have ordered yet. We were waiting for you to arrive so that we can all order at the same time," my dad said, breaking the tension of the moment.

I picked up my menu and started looking in the pancake and waffle section. *Why didn't Daddy tell me over the phone that Mom and Vanessa were going to be here?* I thought.

Our waitress came and we all gave her our orders. After she left, my father spoke, "I gathered us all here today because we need to talk about the riff-raff that has been happening over the past two weeks." He continued. "First of all, we all need to apologize to Truly for ganging up on her. We didn't allow her to tell her side of the story or whatever was going on with Terrell before we jumped to our own conclusions."

They began to apologize one after the other. My father continued, "I know this: we didn't know what happened to Terrell nor did we know his intentions. Bu—"

I cut him off. "His decision had nothing to do with me directly. I never ever talked to him outside of the times he came to the house." I stated, pleading my case to my mother and sister.

"See Vanessa, Pam. I didn't think that Truly would do

something like that. Terrell is the one who had the issue. Truly is not the enemy; she is our family, and we need to put all of this behind us."

Vanessa was the next to speak, "Truly, I honestly want to say sorry. I guess my pride was hurt. And that made me act unreasonable and just downright evil."

I smiled and nodded at my sister. My mother began to speak, "Truly, I know that our apologies can't take away what we have done but we are really sorry."

"With that said," Dad began, "I… we, your mother and I, are asking that you move back home. I don't want you paying any rent right now. I want you to keep saving your money until we have sat down and executed a plan for you to move out."

The waitress appeared, shifting the subject off of me to the food. I agreed with my father that I would move back home, but there was still some uneasiness in my gut about the entire situation. Although my sister and my mother were sorry and I believed them, I still had to live with the fact that I was my sister's understudy.

When we said our good-byes, I hugged and kissed my dad. I asked him to give me a couple of days before I returned home. He agreed and told me to give him a call whenever and for whatever reason.

I decided to make a few runs before work. I received a call from Lily. I enjoy talking to her, even if for just a moment.

She told me about the orientation this weekend at the

studio. It is mandatory because she wanted to get everyone's schedule together in order to begin practicing full-time next month for the charity event. She informed me that she gave Vanessa a call and that she was looking forward to working with us both. I hung up the phone. *I am Vanessa's understudy.* I snapped out of my daze when the cashier asked me, "Paper or plastic?"

"Plastic, please."

# Six

*I was sitting in a field of daisies. I was about three years old. I was playing alone in this wide, open field when my father came and knelt beside me. He had the most beautiful smile on his face. I felt the warmth of the sun. He plucked one of the daisies from the ground beside me and handed it to me. He ruffled the curls on the top of my head as if he were petting a fluffy puppy. I watched him walk away. I was sitting with the daisy that my father gave me when I heard a loud noise. It frightened me but for some reason I didn't cry. But I could see the terror on my face because the noise was so loud, unexpected and disturbing. The next thing I saw was my mother pushing a lawn mower through the field of daisies I was sitting in. I watched her go up and down, back and forth over the field I claimed as my own. I began to cry.*

I woke up a lot more concerned than I ever was before. This was the second dream I had of my mother after which I awoke feeling cold and eerie. I grabbed my journal and wrote down this dream.

I hadn't danced at all since the auditions. I didn't know if we were going to do any dancing today, but to be prepared, I got up and stretched, which my back greatly appreciated.

At work, I told Casey about what happened over breakfast and that I was going back home at the request of my father. She didn't want me to go back home because she said she actually liked waking up and seeing me sprawled out on her sofa. She told me not to hesitate to come back *when* I needed to. Casey always spoke her mind. She told me that I *was* going to be back because, "No disrespect, but your mother and your sister are *s-s-snakes.*" She said it just like that.

I left work and headed straight to the studio. When I arrived, I was greeted by Lily. She pointed to a chair in one of the dance rooms for me to have a seat. She was wrapping up a mixed class of mostly little girls, with a few boys. This class was a lot more advanced than the other class I saw. This group was a lot more serious about the art, and it was obvious that they weren't beginners. I was more intrigued by the boy dancers than the girls. Out of nowhere, I had a thought from my heart enter into my mind, *If I had a son, would he dance?*

The meeting was at 6:00 p.m. It was around 5:30 p.m. when the class ended. I joined Lily in the hall as she sent the children off with their parents.

"How long have those children been dancing?" I asked her, when the last one was out of sight.

"Oh, I would say about three to five years. Many of them have been here, or somewhere else, since the age of four. Some of the boys have been dancing since four and they are nine, ten years old now. They are very graceful young men, not just in their dance, but behavior and attitude. It is my belief that dance helps a man get in touch with his gentle side."

"I agree."

"Those children you saw will be doing a dance for the charity event."

"They will? I would love to see that!" I said.

"Yeah, but I have to start them *really* early because they are children and don't have control of their circumstances. Some of them wake up and decide they don't want to dance anymore, sometimes their parents decide they don't want to bring them anymore, for whatever reason. Some have moved to another state in the middle of practice. So, what I have done over the years is recruit more children than I need so when performance day comes I'm not standing there with my tail tucked between my legs."

"What happens if they all show up for the performance?" I asked.

"Then they all get to perform. If they don't all show up I'm still doing fine. Since we have gotten such an early start, any adjustments that need to be made can happen in enough time."

Lily handed me a bottle of water before taking a seat at her desk, "What are you doing here so early? The meeting isn't for another thirty minutes."

"I know, I just wanted to come and hang out, see how you are doing."

"That's lovely Truly, thank you. It's nice to know someone is thinking about me," she said.

I smiled at her and we sat in silence for a few seconds before a thought came to my mind. "What do you think about dreams?"

"Dreams like the ones you have at night, or goals?" she asked.

"Well, both. I would be interested in what you thought about both if you wanted to share that with me. But I was talking about dreams you have at night."

"What about them? What is it that you are trying to understand? I do believe in dreams. I believe some dreams are God's way of talking to us."

"That makes sense but these dreams don't seem like they are very *godly* dreams. Lately, they have been about my parents and me. I see myself and my parents but there seems to always be a conflict of interest. I feel like my mother is distant from me in my dreams."

"Dreams can also be an unconscious way of expressing what is going on in our life at the moment," she advised. "Are you and your mother having a dispute?"

"Actually, we are. But I feel like I have been disputing with my mother all my life. I don't feel like I fit in. My father and I get along better than my sister and mother and I do. I just don't relate to them."

"Maybe God is trying to tell you something pertaining to your mother. Not just your mother, but your life. You know, I don't think it's about your mother at all," Lily said, changing her mind.

"I think those dreams are about you and the direction of your life."

I looked up from the ground and at her. "That's just it. I don't know the direction of my life."

"Exactly!" She threw up her hands in the air. "If you knew, then why would He need to reveal it to you? I think you're special, Truly. I think there is more coming to you than you think. You just need to stick in there, seek the Lord more, and pay attention, especially to those dreams."

"I've started writing my dreams in a journal because they have been so mysterious."

"That's a start. Be patient in getting the answer. It will come in due time."

The telephone on her desk rang. I watched her talk into the receiver and take notes on a pink notepad. My eyes began to wander around her office. There were a lot of items that I saw before, but there was a picture on a bookshelf that I never noticed before. It was a picture of Mark with a woman. It shocked me as many questions began to roam through my mind about who this woman was. Where is she now?

Lily was still talking on the phone. I got up from the chair, walking toward the costume room. I peered in quickly before turning to the dance room that was across the hall. I walked in, looking around. There was a handbook called, "Every Dancer's Guide." I opened it and began to read when all of a sudden I heard, "Truly! Can you watch my daughter for just a second?"

I turned around startled. It was Mark. He scared me, but I was more startled at the fact that he just asked me to watch his daughter.

"Uh, sure, yes?" I said.

"Truly, this is Istas. Istas, this nice lady is Truly. She's gonna watch you while I go to the office and talk to Nana. I'm just going to be in the other room." I felt that he was explaining this more to me then he was to Istas.

I looked at her as she looked at me, all the while sucking on a lollipop.

"Istas. What an awesome name," I said, trying to break the ice. "You know that is a Native American name. I know that because I danced with a girl once whose name was Istas."

"I know. I'm Indian," she said, licking her lollipop.

"How old are you?"

"I'm four."

This was the most awkward I've ever felt with a child. She wasn't just any child; she was the child of Mark.

She broke the silence and said, "My mommy is Indian."

"Is that right, your mommy is an Indian?" I asked, right before Vanessa walked in.

"Who is this little girl?" she asked.

"I'm Istas."

"She's Mark's daughter. I'm just watching her for

him. He is in the office talking to his mother."

She looked back and forth at the two of us, "This is Mark's daughter? Interesting."

Vanessa bent down and began talking to Istas. As they were talking, Lily walked into the room. Istas ran to Lily and she greeted her granddaughter with multiple kisses. Then Mark walked in with some red roses in his hand. He walked up to Vanessa and I and said, "This delivery guy just gave me these flowers to give to you."

Mark handed me five red roses. There was a card attached that said, "From your secret admirer. Still thinking about you."

"Who would send you flowers?" Vanessa asked.

"I have no idea who could be secretly admiring me," I answered, ignoring her attitude. I thanked Mark for making sure I got my gift. We began talking about the lovely bright red color of the roses.

"So Mark, I met your daughter. She is a very sweet girl. You have done a good job with her. You know, I sometimes work at a children's camp over the summer. I would love to bring you information about the camp. I think Istas would love it," Vanessa said.

My sister is so full of herself. She volunteered two summers ago at that children's camp and has had an excuse for why she has been too busy to go back ever since.

I watched for the rest of the meeting as Vanessa did everything she could to engage Mark in conversation. I stood by as she laughed at every joke and used every opportunity to touch him. Even though I was bothered by her behavior towards Mark, I could *really* feel jealousy arising when she and Lily talked. Even though I had someone admiring me, I was secretly admiring him.

The meeting wrapped up. Since it was the second week of August and roughly four months until the event, we agreed that we would start off practicing twice a week. As the date got closer, we would meet more often, and for longer. Lily dismissed us. I stopped at the restroom before pulling my keys from my oversized purse. I walked out the front door and there were Mark and Vanessa, exchanging numbers. I continued towards my car when Mark said, "It's okay if you're in a hurry. I'll say it for you, good-bye Truly. It was a pleasure talking with you today."

"My sister gets like that sometimes. Just ignore her, I do," Vanessa said.

I waved good-bye, walking to my car, I got in, did a u-turn and drove the opposite direction.

I laid awake that night. I didn't know why I was so frustrated. I didn't have any right to be upset that Mark wasn't available. Besides, he had a child and he had a wife or girlfriend, whoever that woman in the picture was I'm not sure. One thing I was relieved about is that Vanessa couldn't get her hands on him because he wasn't available. Hah. *So why am I still frustrated?* We have never had any other connection other than the times I've seen him at the studio and the one conversation we had at the coffeehouse. I don't know why, but I'm bugging.

Today was the day that I would return to my parent's house. I didn't have much except for some clothing. I left Casey a letter and a gift card to her favorite art supply store. I picked up my two bags and headed out the door. Mark was standing at my car.

"What are you doing here?" I asked.

"I came to help you move," he said.

"How can you help someone move who hasn't told you that they were moving?" I asked.

He tried to grab the two bags from my hand but I resisted.

"How the heck? I never told you... I haven't even spoken one word of where I lived. So how would you know where I stay and that I am moving today? Tell me," I demanded.

"Calm down," he said, gesturing with his hands. "First, I went to your job, the coffeehouse, to visit. You know, grab a cup of coffee. Your friend Casey told me that you weren't working today because you were moving from here back to your parent's house, or something like that."

"Sooo..."

"So, Casey told me the address, and I came by to help you. She said you didn't have anyone to help. I want to help, that's all. I didn't want to just show up at the apartment door, so I decided to stay down here and wait for you. I'm glad I did. I can't imagine how you would have reacted if I knocked on the door."

"That's nice of you and all," I said, releasing my bags to him, "but I don't think a married man should be showing up at the apartment of the understudy even if it's to help her move her two bags."

"Wait, married? What makes you think I'm married?"

"Your daughter told me."

"And what exactly did my daughter say?"

"She said her momma was Indian. Also, I saw the picture of you and her in your mother's office. You're not fooling anyone!"

"What's up with the attitude? Why do you always seem so uptight?" he asked.

"I'm not the one with the baby and the wife trying to holler at his dance partner. You got a lot of nerve," I said as I opened the passenger car door. "You can put my bags in the back seat. Thank you."

He gently placed my bags in the back seat and closed the door.

"This is my fault. I should have never showed up here. Miss, you have a good day."

He pulled his keys from his back pocket. Before getting into his car he said, "My wife is dead. I don't know what my daughter told you, but she has been gone for a few years now."

Mark jumped into his car and drove away. He left me standing there feeling like I needed a crane to lift my jaw off the ground.

I got home about three o'clock. I threw some clothes into the laundry, showered, then sat down in my favorite chair to watch some television. I'm not going to lie; it felt good to be back at home. I hoped the feeling could last as long as I was a resident of my parent's home.

I pretty much laid on the couch the entire afternoon dozing off. When I woke up from one of my naps I looked up and my dad was in his chair watching TV. I looked up at the clock on the living room wall. It was a little after 6:00 p.m. My mother was in the kitchen. I asked Dad where Vanessa was and he said, "In her room." Someone knocked on the door. My mother answered. She appeared in the living room with five roses in her hand and a box of chocolate.

"Maybe Terrell came to his senses. Vanessa! Come downstairs."

A few moments later, Vanessa was standing in the living room with the rest of us." My mother handed Vanessa the gift, "A delivery guy showed up with this stuff but not sure who he worked for. He just handed me this stuff and left," my mother explained to Vanessa. "At least it's a start. Terrell has a lot of making up to do."

"You called me downstairs for this? Those are for Truly," she said shoving the gifts back at my mother.

"How do you know?" my mother asked her. Vanessa, aggravated, stomped back upstairs.

I jumped up from the couch taking my things from her

hand. "This does say my name," I said.

"Who is it from?" Dad asked, now very attentive.

"I don't know. The card says 'From your secret admirer. Are you thinking about me yet?' The first time he sent one rose to my job. The second time he sent five roses to the studio. And now he sent me five more roses with chocolates. I don't have any idea who this is," I said.

My mother interjected, "I think it's from Terrell. And if you keep it, Truly, that is not right."

"We don't know if it's from Terrell," my dad said. "She did say she has received something from this person before."

I took my things to my room. I placed the five flowers in the vase with the six other flowers my secret admirer gave me. The first one was wilted, but the beauty of the others made up for it. My secret admirer had now sent me eleven red roses. I laid the card with the others on my night stand. I sat down on my bed with my box of chocolates, "Terrell is not sending me this stuff. He is not this charming." I laughed as I bit into the chocolate covered cherry candy.

Now that I knew what my practice schedule at the studio would be, I went back to work full-time. I had taken quite a few days off because of all the things going on with my family and the dance studio. After the orientation at the studio, I felt that I gained a sense of control in my life again. I went back to work the day after Mark revealed to me that his wife was deceased.

I made sure that Casey and I were working on the same day. Since we weren't living together anymore I couldn't just go back home and tell her how mad I was at her. So I had to give it to her at work.

"Casey, what did you think you were doing sending Mark to the house without telling me?"

I whispered in her ear.

"I'm sorry, you said you wanted that to be non-fat?" she asked a customer who was ordering.

Once she got the order, she brought me the customer's cup, "She said she wanted a shot of caramel in that, too."

"Don't pretend you didn't hear me, girl," I said.

"I had to do it. You know you like him. You deserve to be happy, too," Casey said.

"Brittany, your single-shot, non-fat caramel latte is ready," I called out, before turning to Casey again.

"I appreciate you doing that but you could have at least told me first. I completely embarrassed myself there. I basically accused him of trying to cheat on his wife with me."

"He's married?" Casey asked.

"No. I thought he was because his daughter said that her mommy was Indian. I didn't know, but his wife is deceased."

"Oh, that's bad. What'd you say to him?"

"I can't even repeat it. I don't remember, I was just

going off. What do you think? I messed it up. Did I mess up my chance of even becoming his friend?" I asked.

"No, I wouldn't say that."

"Why not? Why do you sound so confident, like you've talked to him or something?"

Casey's eyes grew wide and her mouth closed, something was up. "What did you do now?" I asked, following her into the back.

"Okay, calm down. I called him later that night to find out how it went, and he told me what happened without going into much detail."

"So, you have his number? Why are you doing all this behind my back?"

"Like I said, I had to. I did it as your friend. There is something about that guy. I see the way you melt every time he comes around. You're too passive."

"And you're too aggressive."

"He came here that day looking for you. He said he was coming to get a cup of coffee, but I knew he really wanted you because that's the first thing he asked was, "Does Truly work today?"

"He did?"

"Yes. So, I sent him to my apartment because you told me what time you were leaving. We exchanged numbers, and I told him to call if he had trouble finding the place."

"So, he actually came looking for me, huh?"

"Yes girl, don't blow this."

We looked at the front counter and there were two customers, indecisive about what they were going to order. We made our way back to the front, but before we could take our positions behind the counter, Casey said, "Oh, and he'll be up here in an hour so that you can apologize."

"Casey!"

I didn't have enough time to wring her neck because a rush of people came in. We had a steady crowd for about forty-five minutes. After the place calmed down I started cleaning when Mark walked in. We made eye contact as he came closer. *He looks so good,* I thought.

The closer he came towards the counter the faster my heart beat.

"Hey Truly, how are you feeling today?" he asked.

"I'm cool. Thanks," I replied.

"Casey told me to stop by. You want to talk?"

"Yes, she did. I do want to talk." Pointing to a table in the back, "Just have a seat over there and I'll be there in a minute."

Casey told me that she would cover the counter while I spoke with him. I brought him a coffee on me as a peace offering. I apologized for the way that I acted the day before. He accepted my apology. I told him what his daughter said about her mother and how she spoke of her. He explained to me that since she was old enough to understand, he talked to her about her mother. He told me that his wife was Native American and explained that they got married really young; at the age of twenty-three. They both loved to dance, and in fact met at the Academy Dance. He said he didn't know her long before marrying her, but knew that she was the one for him. There was even talk about her taking over the Academy Dance once they married. Two years later, they found out they were pregnant with Istas. After giving birth to their daughter the celebration of the life of their newborn was cut short when they found out that she had cancer in its rarest form. She didn't win the battle. Mark said that he buried his wife only six months after their baby was born. I asked him questions to try to get a sense of who this woman was. He explained to me that the charity event we were practicing for was in memory of his deceased wife. The charity dance show is in its third year. The event is to raise funds for cancer research. Mark wanted to dance a *pas de deux* this year in honor of his wife. I asked him why he didn't inform us that this is what we were auditioning for. He told me that he didn't want to distract people from their performance at the auditions, so he waited to disclose this information after the dancers were chosen.

I didn't want our conversation to end, but I was on still on the clock to work a few more hours. As I escorted Mark out, I saw Casey giving me the thumbs up. I thanked him for sharing his story with me. We hugged and I told him I would see him at the next practice.

Casey and I giggled the rest of the evening about

Mark and the guy from the art gallery she was beginning to see.

We locked up the shop and hugged. As I was pulling away, Casey stuck her head out of her car window and said, "You deserve to be happy, too." I nodded and smiled at her in agreement then drove home.

# Seven

*The little girl I was embracing was indescribably beautiful. She looked about six years old. We were laughing and hugging. There seemed to be a deep connection between the two of us.*

*She jumped out of my lap and began dancing. She had on a leotard, tutu, stockings, and ballet shoes as she danced in front of me. Suddenly, a male's hand touched my shoulder. I embraced it, looking above my shoulder, completely in love.*

I entered this dream into my journal. The date was October 21, 2010. We have had over three months of practicing, with barely two months left to rehearse for the charity event. Today, I felt overwhelmed. I felt like I just needed a break.

I wasn't doing nearly as much as Vanessa was doing. On top of her practicing for her solo dance with Mark, she had modeling gigs and fashion shows she traveled for. Me… I had nothing but a pair of ballet shoes.

I was sitting in the kitchen reading when my mother came in.

"Hey Truly, I was going to start dinner. Let me know when you're finished, I'll come back."

"No you're fine. I was just finishing up anyway." She began pulling out pots and pans.

"What's the occasion?" I asked.

"No occasion. I just feel like cooking for your father tonight. You know he does all the cooking. He came in from a long day, so I thought I could help him by taking care of dinner. What you reading?"

"I don't know, this old book called *Winter's Tale* by Mark Helprin. It was on Dad's bookshelf. I grabbed it because I was bored."

"Your dad, I love him so much. You make sure, Truly, when you settle down, you find someone as great as your Dad," she said.

"How did you meet Dad, Mom?"

"He was actually a blind date."

"No way."

"Yes. Some of my friends were friends with his college buddy. They set us up. I didn't like your dad at first. He was too innocent looking, too nice. I liked a boy I could get into a little trouble with, a roughneck. But the longer we hung out, the more I fell for him."

"Dad is a really nice guy. So he's been like that forever, huh?" I asked.

"As long as I have known him, yes, he has."

"I know what you mean about hanging with someone long enough they grow on you."

"Is there someone you like, Truly?" she asked.

"Yeah… well, sort of. One day I think I like him, then the next day I don't. I try not to think about him, but I do. I guess you would call that liking him."

"I would," she said, stirring something into a pot. "Why don't you just tell him you like him and get it over with? All this time he could be feeling the same way you do. Both of ya'll fiddling 'round each other and got the same emotions. So who is this guy?"

"Who, Beanie?"

"Who?"

"His real name is Mark. I just call him that. I've been secretly calling him that since the day I laid eyes on him."

"So he doesn't he know you call him that," she chuckled.

"Naw. It's an inside thing."

"Truly, that sounds kind of stalker-ish."

"Shut up, Mom," I said, laughing.

"Seriously why do you call him that? What is a 'Beanie' anyway?"

"Beanie is slang of course," I said.

"Of course."

"It is someone who you really dig. Like that person is the coolest."

"But why Beanie?" she said, still confused.

"Don't you agree? If you think of an actual beanie its like a small hat that clings to your head. Wouldn't you want to cling to Dad like a beanie clings to someone's head? You just can't get any closer than that."

She just stood there staring at me. "You gotta be kidding me?"

"You're old. You don't get it!" I joked.

"Oh is that it? I'm old. No you kids are just making up stuff that doesn't make sense. Show me where that is in the dictionary. Go get your Dad's dictionary," she said pointing towards his office.

It's in the dictionary but not the one you're thinking of."

"And what dictionary is that?"

"The urban dictionary."

"Girl get out! The urban dictionary. I am done with this conversation," she said.

The both of us were now laughing.

"So tell me, what does he look like?"

"He is a black guy, light-brown skin. No blemishes. He is perfect... at least he is to me. And he dances."

My mother stopped dicing the tomatoes, turned and looked at me, "What did you say this Beanie's real name was?"

"Mark," I said.

"Mark, hmmm," she said sheepishly, turning her back to me. I rose up from my chair.

"Mom, you act as if you know something about him."

"And you said he dances?"

"Yes."

"That's funny because Vanessa just went out tonight on a date with a Mark from the Academy Dance studio. Isn't that where both of you girls dance?"

I looked at her.

"Oh. That is him, isn't it?" she asked.

My mother opened the oven, brushed the tomatoes into a pan of salmon and placed it inside saying, "I guess she got to him first."

"I guess she did." I grabbed my book and excused myself to my room.

I cried the entire drive to Casey's house. I pulled up and her car was there. When I got myself together enough to make my way into her apartment, I couldn't allow myself to tell her what I just found out. She would do two things: tell me that she told me so and that I should have gone for him. And also she would have wanted to find Vanessa and tell her what she really thought about the situation. I didn't want any of those things to happen, so I wiped my tears and pretended that I was over there to say hello.

# Eight

I stayed at Casey's that night. I didn't want to be there when Vanessa got home. I avoided her every chance I got. Over the next week I showed up at the house when she wasn't there to get clean clothes. But I presented myself enough so my Dad didn't know I was staying in between home and Casey's. There were a few times Vanessa had to miss practice because she didn't make it back into town in time. That's when I would show up. I asked Lily when Vanessa was scheduled to be into practice. When she told me, I made sure I missed that practice. I rescheduled with Lily to practice alone. She told me that Beanie wouldn't be there, but she would help me with what I missed. Today, I wasn't feeling like doing anything at all, not making a cup of coffee or dancing; I pushed through anyway.

I got to the studio and Lily caught me up on the steps that I missed. Once I caught on, I asked her to leave me alone. I stood there with my reflection before me. My eyes gazed first at my hips, how they curved outward. My waist was smaller than my hips. My stomach didn't overlap my waist, it was perfectly tone. I moved up to my breasts which were a nice size, right up to my collar bone, to my chin. I raised my hand gently touching the cheek of my dark brown skin. I rubbed my cheek in a circular motion as if applying make-up, but there was no blush here. All I saw was brokenness, confusion. I looked at my forehead, then up to the top of my head where my hands followed. I placed both of my hands flat onto the top of my head; smoothing down my hair that was no longer than my ears. My hands fell to my sides.

I raised my arms into the *bras bra* position, both my arms were down and rounded with both hands placed in front of my hips, my fingers almost touching. As I felt my body take on this position, my mind went blank. I began to dance like there was no tomorrow. I put every emotion into my dance: fear, anger, uncertainty, stress. I could never remember performing like this ever before. Where was my life going? Why was I created?

As I went to leap, I felt hands grasp my waist, lifting me from the ground into the air. The body melted to the shape of my body as we danced the same rhythm. I looked and saw it was Mark. He spun me around. I felt like I was dancing in my dream. But this was not like a dream I could go write in my journal. This was reality.

He turned me around and the front of our bodies was touching. I looked into his eyes, overwhelmed by his touch. We were so close, I knew the next thing we were going to do was kiss. He pulled me close, embraced me, and I melted in his arms. We stared at one another until he let me out of his grasp. *He didn't kiss me. Why didn't he kiss me?*

I gathered myself asking, "Why did you do that?"

"We've practiced many times, but I've never seen you dance like that before. Truly, you just put your heart and soul into that dance. You dance like you were born to. I'm not just saying that. If I would have known you could dance like that, you wouldn't have been anybody's understudy," he said.

I turned away from him, confused.

He continued, "I've desired to get to know you since I laid eyes on you. I've tried everything I could but you're pretty tough, like you are guarding yourself from something or someone."

I walked to a chair in the back of the room and sat down. I looked at him and asked, "When you say you 'desire' me. What exactly does that mean?"

He paused for a moment then answered, "I don't know."

"What do you mean I don't know? How can you use a strong word as 'desire' and not know why?" I asked.

He replied, "Truly, sometimes we don't have all the answers, at first. And that's okay. This is when we just trust God like never before." I sat slouched over in my chair pondering the truth he just shared with me. But` soon confusion crept in, "Then why would you go on a date with Vanessa if you had this so-called desire for me? Why didn't you just ask me?"

Mark came closer. He answered, "Date! I never took that girl on a date! There was one time she joined my mother and I for dinner. It was after practice one day when my mother and I were talking about going out for dinner. So my mother invited her to come. I think she tried to hint to me all night that she was interested, but I played it cool."

He grabbed my hand and stood me on my feet, "I don't know where things are gonna go from here but can we both agree that we are friends?"

"Agreed," I said.

We gathered our things and he walked me to my car where we exchanged numbers.

"Now I have your number so I don't have to keep stopping by your job. I can just call ya'."

"I would like that," I said.

I got into the car and he closed the door behind me. As soon as I could get my key into the ignition and my foot on the gas, I raced home. It was time for me to confront Vanessa once and for all.

I pulled up to my house and the lights in the living room were on. I went in and my Mom and Dad were watching television. I grabbed the remote and turned the TV off.

"Hello, honey," my dad said.

I went straight to my mother and started pointing the remote in her face.

"I don't know what problem you have with me, but today it's gonna stop."

"Truly, what's the problem now?" my dad asked.

"She is. Vanessa is. Dad, you act like you don't see the way they treat me. It's like you turn a blind eye to the way they treat me, just so you won't have to deal with her evil self."

"What are you talking about Truly?" my mother started. "You know, I know what this is all about. Admit it, you're jealous of your sister and her career. You don't have anything going for yourself, so you walk around with a dang-o chip on your shoulder, mad at me, mad at her, mad at the *world!*"

"See, that's the problem," I said, pacing back and forth. "You make up this thing that I am jealous of Vanessa so she can feel important. And you go around saying stuff that isn't true so you can keep busy. That's why Dad stays away at work as long as he can. He doesn't want to deal with your evilness."

"If you call me evil again girl—"

As my mother threatened me Vanessa came downstairs. "What's going on?"

I rushed over to her pointing my finger in her face, "Why did you lie and say you went on a date with Mark?"

"I didn't lie, I did go on a date with him," she said.

"No you didn't. He said that you joined him and his mother. Not a date!"

"Is this what this is about? Another guy? You girls have really got to find something else to fight about," Dad said.

"This is not just about another guy, Dad. This is about Mom and Vanessa trying to ruin my life. Vanessa lied and said she went out with this guy that she knew I liked. And Mom helped her do it. Do you know why? All because they think I tried to steal Terrell from her. Terrell didn't want her because she doesn't have anything else to offer but her looks. All she does is talk about herself. You're not all that, and no one cares."

My mother jumped up, "You've gone far enough. We have brought you into this family and treated you like our own daughter, and this is the thanks we get!"

I stopped, "What are you talking about?"

I looked around the room. Everyone stared at me as if I were a complete stranger who walked into their house unannounced. I looked back and forth at my Dad and Mom; my heart now beginning to beat faster and faster.

"What do you mean 'brought me into this family?" Silence. "S-so…y-you're saying I'm adopted? So you are saying you are not my real mother and father?"

I struggled to get the words out. My stomach felt queasy, I couldn't breathe.

Everyone continued to stare in silence. I looked at each one of them staring back at me. I was right, I am a *stranger.*

I made eye contact with my mother but only briefly. She could barely look at me; her face full of dread, her body language portraying regret. She stood awkwardly frozen in place. Tears started uncontrollably falling down my face while inside I was screaming to my mother, "Please answer me!" I was too weak to form the words.

My dad finally arose from his trance and took a hold of me. He embraced me as the tears got harder and stronger. I screamed loudly in his arms, "I don't get it!... I'm so confused... I'm adopted?"

I felt so much pain, hurt, betrayal!

My mother slowly walked over to us and placed her hand on my back. My crying turned to anger as I snatched away from my dad's grasp lashing out.

"Don't touch me, Pamela! Don't ever touch me!"

The look of dread was back on her face. Vanessa was sitting on the couch crying.

"I'm adopted!" I started pacing around yelling, "I'm adopted. Are you serious!"

"Truly! Please calm down," Pamela said, crying.

"That's it! You did it! You got exactly what you wanted for all these years, to get me out of *your* family. You don't have to pretend anymore Pa-me-la."

"Truly that's not what I wanted. I..." Pamela tried to explain herself but I didn't want to hear it. I exploded upstairs to my room, my dad and Pamela following behind me. I grabbed my suitcase, duffel bag, whatever I could find to stuff things into.

"Truly where do you think you're going? You can't keep running every time our family has a problem," my dad said.

I stopped packing my bag, "*Our* family? No this is *your* family," pointing my fingers at his chest. I kept slamming clothes into my bags.

"You know this is my fault," Pamela cried. "I didn't mean for you to find out like this Truly, I really didn't. I was just upset and if I could take it back I would."

I sat down on my bed. I couldn't stand it. My emotions were all over the place: sad, then angry, then lonely. I couldn't do anything else but cry.

"Truly, I know you're hurting right now. I understand that. There is nothing your mother and I can say to erase what happened but—"

I looked up at them with the last bit of strength I had and said, "You understand? You can't even imagine the hurt that I am feeling right now. My life has been nothing but a lie. Please just get out."

"Okay." My Dad grabbed Pamela's arm and pulled her out of the room.

Once I gained a little more strength I grabbed as much as I could to take with me, throwing handfuls of my belongings into my car. Vanessa stood in the doorway of the kitchen quietly watching me come back and forth. As I came back in from my car, Vanessa asked, "Truly would you like me to help you?"

Instantly I stopped dead in my tracks and gave her the coldest silent look. She got the point as she turned away, going into her room, closing the door.

After stuffing my front, back seats, and trunk with as

much of my things as possible, I jumped in and sped away. I didn't exactly know where I was going. I drove to my job, stopping then driving away. I didn't want to talk to anyone. I drove to the next closest coffeehouse to use the Internet. I pulled out my laptop and booked a motel room. I got to the motel room. The only things I brought to my room were my computer and my purse. I purposely left my phone in the glove box. I dropped my things to the floor as if dropping heavy bricks. I flopped down on the bed. My thoughts were racing. The same scene kept replaying over in my mind. I saw Pamela standing there uttering the words that would forever change my life. I gathered my thoughts as tears started to stream down my face again. *No I am not going there again.* I sat up, quickly drying my face with my hands. My thoughts continued, *I'm shutting everyone out. It feels like I've been betrayed by the whole world.*

I laid on the bed, crying myself to sleep.

I woke up this morning in a complete blur. My eyes were swollen and puffy from crying on and off since yesterday. A couple of days had gone by since I checked into my room eating nothing but take out when I could eat. I haven't talked to anyone, not even Casey. As of right now there is no one I can really trust. I don't even trust myself. I don't quite know who I am.

When I finally got out of bed for the day, I went to the

bathroom to put a warm towel on my face. I turned on the light, it blinded me. The bathroom light was the first light I'd seen all day. The entire room I kept dark—depressing. I grabbed a face towel off of the sink and began running warm water over it. I stared at myself in the mirror looking at my features. Once I thought my hair came from Pamela and my nose from my dad, Brian. I softly pulled down on my hair then touched my nose. I have the features of a man and woman I never ever laid my eyes upon. A man and a woman whose names I didn't know.

I bet I have an entire family of cousins, aunts, uncles, grandparents, and probably brothers and sisters I don't know. My curiosity turned to frustration. I need answers. I'm tired of asking questions and not getting any answers. I decided that Brian had some explaining to do. I trusted him.

I took a shower, got dressed and ran to the car to get my phone. Sitting in the driver's seat I scrolled through my phone at all my missed calls. I ignored them all going straight to Brian's number. His phone rang only once. He picked up immediately, "Hello, Truly. How are you doing honey? It's so good to hear from you."

"Hello. Can you meet somewhere? I'm not meeting you at your house."

"Yes! I'm not at the house. Here's where to meet me."

I grabbed a pen and paper and wrote down the address he gave me.

"I love you honey."

"I'll see you soon." Brian told me to meet him at the hotel that was a few blocks from the campus he taught at. Our family had stayed there before for conferences he spoke at, and the school supplied him with a courtesy room.

I got up to the door, 232, and knocked. Brian opened the door; the lights were dim and the TV was off. It looked as if he hadn't shaved in a while.

"Are you staying here? Where's Pamela?" I said peering behind him to see if she was in there, my body becoming very tense.

"She's at home. Come in." He said. I felt my shoulders relax.

"I came here yesterday. I really needed to have some space since that night to think. What happened was so unfortunate. I'm not going to lie I was very angry with the way Pamela told you that you were adopted. I don't know how long I'll be here… I… I just need to clear my mind."

"Oh," I said.

He continued, placing his hand on my shoulder, "I didn't know when you were going to call me. I felt so guilty about you being out there alone. I'm so happy you decided to call me. I am worried about you."

I went there upset with him, but seeing him the way he was, he looked like I felt. He flicked on the light and there were books and clothes all over one of the beds in the room. The covers on the other bed were turned back; I guess he was using that one for sleeping. He went into the bathroom while I went and sat at the desk. There were letters all over the desk. Some were addressed to Pamela and him, while others were addressed to just him. One letter said:

*Dear Brian and Pamela,*

*I got the picture you sent me. Wow! She sure is growing up to be a beautiful girl. She's five years old now. She's starting to look like her father's mother. But it's hard to tell with children, they change so much over the years.*

I didn't read the rest because I just wanted to see who the person writing this letter was. I flipped the letter over on the back. It read, "Love, Cynthia."

I heard the toilet flush in the bathroom before the door swung open. Brian walked up to the desk, "I see you found the letters." He took one off of the desk, plopping onto the bed.

"Cynthia, your real mother, always kept in touch with us. She didn't want to have contact with you, only because she wanted you to have the most normal life possible. Even though she requested that we not tell you, she did want us to keep her updated. We sent her pictures of every birthday, dance recital, everything. Whatever you did, she knew about it. She would write us back when she received the letters and pictures."

He took the letter from my hand and looked at it.

"Yeah this one was when you turned five. We sent her a picture of you. You know that picture we have in the album where you were sitting on the lap of that clown?"

I thought for a moment, then said, "Yeah, I know that one."

"This is her letter in response to ours that we sent her," he said.

"Why did you adopt me? Why did she give me up? Why didn't you just have another child of your own?" I asked, as the questions started pouring out.

"I know you're upset, Truly. But—"

"Truly! Is Truly even my real name? Do you know what this information has done to me? Why didn't you just tell me from the beginning that I was adopted? All this year, I have been trying to figure out what my purpose is. I have felt a void in my life because I just don't fit in. Now ya'll hit me with this. I don't even know who I am."

Tears of hurt and desperation began to fall.

"I understand, I really do. And to find out the way you did was just not right. Believe me, if I could turn back the hands of time, I would have stopped Pamela from saying that."

"Is Vanessa your real daughter?" I asked.

"Yes," he said.

There was silence.

"Vanessa was a hard birth. She gave your mother a lot of trouble. We were ready to have another child, but

Pam, she wasn't so sure if she wanted to try for another. With the doc's advice, it wasn't a bad idea to adopt. I wanted a son."

"So why am I here? Why didn't you get a son?"

"We began looking. We contacted an adoption agency and let them know we wanted to adopt a child. Our case-worker said that there was a lady, Cynthia, who was having a child whom she wanted to put up for adoption. We met with her. We told her what we wanted.

She told us that she was six months along and re-quested not to know the sex of the child. Pam and I stayed in contact with Cynthia. We discussed all the time the benefit of adopting a child that we could raise from birth. But not knowing the sex of the baby was a challenge. Have you ever just felt like you had to do something? I did.

"As I met with Cynthia and saw her get bigger and bigger I got attached to you. After that I didn't care if you were a boy or not. I just couldn't imagine not taking you home with me because you weren't the right gender. I talked to Pam and we agreed that we would take Cyn-thia's baby and raise it as our own, boy or girl. Cynthia called us from the hospital the day she went into labor. We waited for hours until she began delivery and shortly thereafter, into the world you came. The doctor handed us the scissors and Pam and I both cut the umbilical cord. It was obviously a girl! At that point, when I saw you, I didn't care that you weren't a boy. All I saw was that you were mine, truly mine. Your mother and I went there with a name, a different name, but you left the hospital as 'Truly'."

I jumped up and grabbed my Dad by the neck. We hugged for a few minutes, both sniffling and crying. He pulled me off of his shoulder. We were looking face to face. I felt like a child who just got hurt... Daddy was there to comfort me.

His eyes were red from crying, "Truly, just because Pamela and I didn't give birth to you doesn't make you not rightfully ours. More importantly, it doesn't make you insignificant."

"Then why do I feel so insignificant, Dad?"

He sat for a moment in silence staring at me. He then replied, "Your destiny is not dependent upon who your earthly parents are, Truly. All that matters is that you connect with your Heavenly Father. Once you do this... you will find your purpose." I hugged and thanked my dad for his support. I went to the bathroom to wash my face. My new-found mission was to connect with my Heavenly Father. Then I will know my purpose. *How do I do that?* I thought.

My dad called out, "Truly, are you okay?"

"Yes, but I have one more question."

"I'm listening."

I stepped out of the bathroom, "How do I connect with my Heavenly Father?"

He immediately responded, "Through prayer and surrendering your life *fully* to Him. Hold nothing back. He is all that you need."

The rest of the night my dad and I went through the letters that Cynthia had sent him. He ordered us dinner through room service. That night, we didn't leave the room one time. We discussed what my life was going to look like now that I knew what I knew. I asked many more questions. Some he could answer and some he couldn't.

I asked him again, "Why did my mother give me up?"

He said, "That question is something only she can answer."

My dad cleared off the bed with the books and papers for me to sleep on. I hopped into the bed, burying myself under the fluffy covers, and fell fast asleep.

I woke up early the next morning to a phone conversation my father was having with Pamela. I looked around and he was sitting at the desk sipping a cup of coffee he had made from the complimentary supply in the room. The entire room was cleaned. His bed was made up. All the papers that had been scattered everywhere had now disappeared, right along with the fuzzies that were on his face. He had clean clothes on, like he was ready to leave at any moment.

I lay still, so as not to let him know I was listening. I couldn't hear much because he was talking very discreetly, either not to wake me or not for me to hear, probably both. What I did hear was him telling Pam that we all needed to go to family counseling. In between some other words, and what she may have said to him, he told her, "I'm coming back soon."

He got off of the phone and pulled my leg, "I know you didn't bring a change of clothes, but let me take you to breakfast anyway. No one will know you had that on yesterday except me, and the bellhop, and the front desk clerk and the valet. But that's all."

We laughed the entire time during breakfast. I felt like I could place him back on my list of people I could trust. So I decided to tell him the decision I made yesterday. "I am going to look for my real mother. I am going to go look for Cynthia."

"Honey, I don't know if that is a good idea," he said.

"Why not? I mean it's been twenty-three years. It's not like I'm a little kid who will get attached to her or something. I just want to meet her, ask her some questions," I said.

"But I have answered all your questions."

"You have not answered two of my questions. Why did Cynthia give me up and who is my father? I really need to get these questions answered."

"Truly, I know that you are anxious to have these questions answered. But you have to take into consideration Cynthia's feelings and how she would react to her birth daughter unexpectedly contacting her. What if she's not open to meeting you? I would hate for you to experience that kind of rejection." His face full of concern.

"Dad, I understand where you are coming from, I do. But… this is a risk I'm willing to take."

Still very hesitant he said, "Okay… Truly, I want you to know that I am here for you no matter what happens."

"I know."

We went back to the hotel room. He gave me a piece of paper in which he wrote the last three known addresses that Cynthia had used.

"Why did you only give me addresses?" I asked.

"Remember I told you we only communicated by mail. This is why I was trying to warn you, Truly. There is no way that you can call her. You would have to write her a letter or literally go to where she is to talk to her."

"If that's what I have to do," I said shrugging my shoulders.

"What? Write the letter?" he asked.

"No. I'm gonna go there," I said abruptly.

Breathing very heavily, he said, "I think this is a very abrupt decision you're making. I'm not going to tell you not to go because you are an adult. I am going to ask if we can agree that you will sleep on this decision?"

"Yes. I will sleep on it."

He kissed me multiple times on my forehead and told me to call whenever and for whatever I needed. I left my dad feeling better about our relationship but still planning to never talk to Pamela again. Every time I thought of her I wanted to punch something.

I had taken in more than enough for the day. Like I said, I was going to sleep on it. I had the entire day with nothing to do. My plan was to go back to my motel room and relax.

After a day of shopping, swimming at the motel pool, and eating some of my favorite strawberry-vanilla ice cream after dinner, I laid down to go to sleep.

*Am I sure I want to do this? What if Dad is right? What if she totally rejects me because I just showed up without warning? What am I going to do?*

I woke up this morning three days after leaving from the place I once called home. It felt good to be on my own for a change. I got up and got dressed; no one was in the room but me. I had space to think, be loud, be quiet, be myself without anyone questioning me. There was no one else's life for me to look at and wonder what I was going to do with my own. I could just go from here with no comparisons; it was just me, God, and my instincts. There was no one downstairs telling me when to eat dinner. I wasn't sharing a bathroom with Vanessa. And the best part was there was no mother to get into petty arguments with… hmm… *no mother.*

The awesome feeling of freedom quickly left as I snapped back to reality. I was in a motel room because the only mother I know isn't the woman who gave me birth. I'm at the moment of making the most important decision of my life. I grabbed my purse and headed out the door to go see Lily. It felt good to be in the position to make my own decisions for my life even though I didn't quite know the entirety of those decisions yet. But I once again did something someone else wanted me to do. I kept my agreement with my dad: I did sleep on the decision to go try to find my birth mother. Now I'm going to do what I want to do; I am going to try and find Cynthia.

I got to Academy Dance where Miranda was teaching some of the kids that Lily usually teaches. She waved at me as I passed by. I made my way back to Lily's office and there was a guy in a suit seated on the other side. I waited outside the door for some time until the man came out. He nodded hello, and I watched him walk out of the front door. Lily called to me to come in. She began talking about the meeting that she had with the guy who just left. I felt honored that she shared this information with me. She offered me information that I didn't even ask for. Lily was one of those people who was still on my list of those I could trust.

And I think I was on her list as well.

She told me that she was starting to look for someone to take over Academy Dance. She said that no man had ever run the place, but the one who just left was a good prospect. She said that she was ready to retire from the company and start taking care of her paralyzed husband full-time, to just be a wife and grandma.

I spoke to her about having to go out of town and not being able to make the next few practices. She said that it would be okay since we had already practiced the entire dance. And I was the understudy anyway. She didn't see any lack in Vanessa and thought that she was a beautiful girl. She agreed that we still had a couple of months left to practice and she would let us know closer to the date when we would have to pick up and start meeting more frequently. I didn't want to tell anyone why I was leaving, but I had to tell her. I requested that she not discuss this information with Vanessa if she asked. With concern in her face, she gave her word. I explained everything to her. I told her how I found out that I was adopted. I told her some of what my father told me while I was with him. And I told her that I *had* to figure this entire situation out. I asked, "Has Mark come by here today?"

"Naw, haven't seen that boy today," she said.

"I would have liked to let him know that I was leaving. You know, since we are dance partners. It would have been courteous if I could have told him without just leaving abruptly. But I don't want everybody to know yet. I don't want anyone trying to talk me out of this," I explained.

"Oh, don't worry about him. He is a pretty understanding guy. I'll just let him know you took a short vacation."

I got up to start gathering my stuff to leave. She followed behind me, "Truly, do you have feelings for Mark?" she asked plainly.

"Um... oh... whoa, why do you ask?" I said.

"Just because he seems to talk to me about you a lot. And the last person he talked to me like that about was his wife. I'm not going to lie, I thought he had a thing for Vanessa but the way he's been acting, it's you he may have feelings for. I know my son. He starts to act all funny when I mention your name," she said with a smile.

I blushed politely on the outside, but inside there was a parade happening. My emotions were playing the tuba, the horn, and the drums.

She gave me a hug and handed me a map. She said it would be very handy to have. I told her I had my cell phone and she responded, "Batteries die, paper doesn't."

I headed back to my motel. I looked at the three addresses given to me that will eventually lead me to Cynthia's home in Arizona. I pulled out my phone and started doing research on how far Arizona is from Kansas. I found out that I would be driving twenty-four hours to Goodyear, Arizona to find her. I decided to start with the first address on the list.

I looked at the clock and it was a little past 7:00 p.m. Since I decided to leave early in the morning I wanted to get some rest. Within an hour I was packed and in the bed ready for my journey.

The next morning I checked out of my motel room then stopped at the bank. I withdrew enough money to cover my food, gas, and lodging expenses. I drove past the house to find that no one was there, particularly

Pamela. After I found it safe enough to go inside, I grabbed clothes, CDs, some food out of the fridge, and left. I stopped at Casey's home and wrote her a quick note about my trip to Arizona. I didn't tell her why. I wasn't ready to. I called Jeremy at the coffeehouse and told him I had to take an emergency trip out of town. Lastly, I called my dad and let him know I was leaving.

I waited for the car beside me to speed ahead then I merged onto I-35 headed to Oklahoma City, then to I-40 west to Arizona.

# Nine

Seeing the green, spotted patches that are left over after the grass burnt in the Flint Hills, let me know that I'd been driving for a couple of hours. This is the first time I had ever driven out of the state without my parents. The closest I'd ventured to another state without my parents was on a school bus ride to Missouri from Kansas for a field trip in ninth grade.

This moment was bittersweet. The bitter part was the fact that I am traveling over twenty hours to meet a biological mother I didn't know existed, and that she doesn't even know I'm coming. The sweet part of this journey is that I am going to discover a part of me that I never knew existed. My thoughts were a mixture of what my biological mother looks like and thoughts of Mark. It is unfortunate that I had to leave at this time. Even though I felt that we could have possibly started something, I think it's best that I first know who I am before I can love anyone else.

The circumstances that led to my father telling me the truth of who I am, led me to hurry off onto this journey, and now I am feeling the hunger pangs of this decision. I saw an exit sign a couple miles back indicating a rest stop was coming up soon. On the left side of the road I saw rows of trucks parked, and on the right side I saw a restaurant and a gas station. I took a right turn as I decided to eat then fill up my tank before getting back on the road. Eating quickly, I jumped into my car and parked in front of a gas pump. I kept my eyes on a black couple in a SUV behind me, with the effort of trying to ignore the stares of the gentleman across from my pump. When we finally made eye contact, the guy pumping the gas said, "Hello." He was white and had chin length blonde hair.

I said, "Hi," really quickly, trying not to make any eye contact.

"My name is Charlie," he said.

"Hello Charlie," giving him a small wave back.

"You from around here?" he asked.

"No I'm a few hours from here, I'm on my way to visit a friend."

"So where are you headed?" he asked.

"To Arizona."

"Whew, way down there! You got a long way to go."

"I know. But believe me it's worth the trip."

"You're not scared to travel alone? If I had a woman as pretty as you are, you wouldn't be traveling alone."

I blushed as I answered with a soft, "Thank you."

Charlie looked back and forth between the gas pump and at me.

I pretended as if I didn't know he was staring, looking at my pump as the last dollar slowly rolled into my tank. I never really cared why the pumps didn't pump faster until today.

He finally spoke up, "I know you don't know me at all so this may seem awkward for me to ask. Is it possible we could exchange numbers?"

The gas finally stopped, and I returned it back to the pump.

Flattered yet curious I asked, "How in the world would we have any type of relationship even if it is a friendship? We are from two different cities," I asked.

He shrugged his shoulders, "I don't know. If it's meant to be it will be, right?"

I agreed with him and we exchanged numbers. He told me he would be in contact soon, got into his car and left.

The weather started to get a little cooler. I opened the back passenger door and started pulling out shirts, socks hair products looking for a sweater. After putting on the sweater I tried to stuff everything back in the bag but couldn't. *How did I get this stuff in here?*

I got everything back in but couldn't zip the top of the bag with the hair product sitting right at the top of the bag. Looking over the entire bag, I unzipped the small pocket on the side of the bag to stuff the products in; I pulled out a picture of Mark and I. One day Lily took pictures of all the dancers so that she could update the website with this year's company. Randomly at practice Lily handed me this picture of Mark and I. When I packed my stuff I made sure to put this picture in my bag.

*I wonder what he is doing. I wonder if he is thinking about me. If Lily did tell him I left, I wonder what he would say.*

I stuffed everything back into the side pocket. When I got back on the road, I sipped on the juice I bought from the gas station and turned the radio up.

I looked back and forth at the road and the radio as I turned the dial trying to find something to listen to. Suddenly this unrecognizable female voice appeared on the radio as people were clapping in agreement to something she just said. I pulled my hand away placing it back on the steering wheel to listen to the unknown female voice:

"I couldn't believe that she did that to me. I couldn't believe that she betrayed my trust. I was right and she was wrong. Therefore I have a right to hold a grudge."

When I heard her say this I reached over turning the volume up, listening more carefully.

"She wronged me and I will never speak to her again. This is what I felt until Jesus started dealing with my heart. Forgiveness—this is what I am going to talk about today. I am going to talk about why is it important to forgive when someone hurts you. The Bible says…" As soon as I heard her say, "The Bible says" I pushed the power button off on the radio. I felt my heart began to pound and my emotions became frustrated, "I'm not forgiving her. She doesn't deserve my forgiveness! Pamela doesn't even deserve one bit of me and I am not going to let her control my life or my emotions any-more! Forget that forgiveness stuff, I don't need to for-give because I don't need her. I can do without her!"

I turned the radio back on changing the station to an-other one I knew was *far* from talking about forgiveness.

I drove a couple of hours longer. I pulled onto the side of the road to stretch my legs. I checked my phone; there was a text message from Charlie. He said it was nice meeting me today. He was looking forward to us talking when I wasn't busy. I placed my phone back onto the passenger seat. I decided not to respond to Charlie. After seeing the picture of Mark and me together I realized how much I liked him. I just wasn't ready to entertain the thought of liking someone else right now.

I got back onto the road to keep it moving. A few more hours passed, and now I had been driving for seven hours. Keeping one hand on the steering wheel, I used my free hand to feel around the seat for my cell phone. When I finally grabbed it, I saw that I had a missed call from my father. I decided that I was going to pull over and call him back. I kept driving until I found a safe place to pull over. I started seeing signs that indi-cated that I would be entering into Oklahoma soon. I came up to a very small town. There were a few houses, a school, and a bar. I thought that this would be a good time to stop so I pulled over. I called my Dad and he answered on the first ring. He said that he was just call-ing to check on me and see if my drive was safe. After telling him that everything was alright, and assuring him that I had everything I needed, we hung up. Before I started back on my journey, I realized it was getting late, and I should start looking for somewhere to sleep for the night. After searching the web on my phone, I found a little bed and breakfast in Oklahoma that I was going to stop at.

I drove for another hour or so when I felt my head begin to nod. I blasted the music really loud to keep myself from falling asleep until I made it to the bed and breakfast. It was very small, definitely not part of any kind of chain. There was a bar that was some ways down the street from the bed and breakfast.

If these little towns didn't have anything else, they had a bar. This one had music blaring and lights flashing out of it. People were hanging outside smoking and drinking beer. I could hear chatter and music up the street, broken up by occasional laughter and the general sounds of people just having fun.

After checking into the bed and breakfast, I came back outside to get some fresh air. I could hear the music from the bar still and it filled my ears and my heart. Even this music, with a slight twang and a heavy drawl lingering in the lyrics, made me want to dance. *I can't remember the last time I have just had fun. I am only twenty-three years old and right now I don't feel like it.*

I walked toward the bar; it looked crowded. On the

outside, it looked small, but as I got closer I could see inside the large glass window. It was way bigger on the inside than it looked on the outside. To the left were people seated at the bar, requesting drinks from two women who were serving like they had the arms of an octopus. Something about the melody of the country music drew me inside the bar. I could see people dancing in boots and cowboy hats in the back of the bar.

I looked over to the dance floor. As the song changed the people on the floor started to move, organizing themselves for a square dance. I stood and watched them twirl their partners around the floor in perfect unison. This wasn't dancing that I was frequently exposed to, but I watched the patterns of their feet and counted the steps in my head. As I mentally danced out their rhythms a gentleman came up and stood beside me.

"You don't look familiar. I come here a lot. I know I haven't seen you here before."

I looked over to see who it was talking to me. This guy was black; he looked like he was in his early thirties. Surprised to see someone almost my age in here that I could relate to, I became more interested in what he had to say. I quickly looked him up and down. He had on a cowboy hat, a creased long sleeve button down shirt tucked into his jeans. His jeans were tightened with a silver-buckled belt and black cowboy boots. We stared at each other until I said, "I'm not from here. I heard the music and stopped by to see what was happening in here."

"That's cool! I'm Derrick." He said sticking out his hand.

"I'm Truly," I said shaking his hand in return.

We both looked back at the dance floor. "So where are you from, Truly?"

"I'm from Kansas. I am just passing through. I'm on my way to see a family member."

He nodded with a smile.

We stood there a few seconds longer before he asked me to dance. "I've never square danced before. I have no idea what I am doing. I would look crazy over there trying to square dance."

"You won't look crazy. If you just do what I tell you to do you will look like everybody else. I mean, think about it. We are all just doing the same steps. I'll help you, c'mon."

I shook my head, "No thanks."

Not taking *no* for an answer Derrick took off his hat sticking his hand out he said, "May I?"

I reluctantly took his hand as he walked me over to the dance floor, "I can't do this," I told him.

He ignored my pleas to not embarrass myself as he escorted me with a smile.

He started dancing and I started to mimic what he was doing the best I could. He looked at me and said, "Now you're gonna do the grapevine like this." He stepped to the right with his right foot. Then stepped to the right with his left foot; crossing his left foot behind his right foot. He kept repeating the grapevine for me until he felt like I really got it. It was very fun. I hadn't laughed like that in a long time.

Once the music stopped he turned to me, "You didn't do so bad for a first timer."

"Yeah well, I am a dancer, sort of. I don't dance country, but I do dance ballet."

"So you do. Show me what you're made of," he said.

"Absolutely not, I can't do that."

He looked at me and said, "You sure say 'can't' a lot."

Derrick ran over to the DJ. The DJ nodded in agreement and started playing this semi-slow-paced music. Derrick ran onto the middle of the dance floor and said, "Now that I have taught you my type of dance, you owe me. You have to teach me your type of dance."

Embarrassed, but determined to show fair exchange for teaching me to square dance, I went up to him. My brain racing thinking of what I could do; doing whatever came to mind. I started off in attention with a *bras bas.* My arms hanging low, forming a circle and my palms facing each other. The crowd starting cheering. Derrick leaned in whispering in my ear, "You got the whole bar cheering! It's not every day we have a ballerina in here with us country folk."

The crowd's gratitude for seeing a new thing sprung up some excitement inside of me. My shyness began to subside as I then went into the *devant,* placing one hand above my head and one arm stretched out from my side. My back foot was bent at an angle while my front leg I swung up and down. Next I moved into elevation beginning and ending each step with a *demi-plié,* half-bending my knees as I elevated across the dance floor.

As I moved across the dance floor I instructed Derrick the correct way to hold his hand in the *demi-plié.*

Everyone in the entire bar was watching us. They cheered as I danced. They laughed when he attempted to do the moves that I taught him. After about ten minutes of showcasing my talent and Derrick being completely willing to look silly, I thanked my partner for the dance and for the great time. I told him that this experience was one that I would always remember, then I walked back to my room at the bed and breakfast and fell fast asleep.

I got up early, showered, ate breakfast, and hit the road. At this point, I have seventeen hours left to drive. I plan on driving the rest of the way until I arrive in Arizona early tomorrow morning.

# Ten

My plans went somewhat as expected. I did arrive in Arizona the next day like I planned, but it was nowhere near early. I arrived in Goodyear, Arizona around 1 p.m. Thank God for my dad who helped me map out where I was going. He helped me determine what motel I was going to stay at each stop. He made it very easy for me. There was one of the motels my Dad found for me that I didn't stay in. Instead, I ended up sleeping in my car. The plan was to drive seventeen hours straight by myself to Arizona. I ended up pulling over at a rest stop and taking a break.

I checked into a motel closest to the first of the three addresses that my Dad had for Cynthia. After I moved all of my bags into my room, I started to feel anxious. The entire drive I had everything planned out like what I was going to say to her once I met her. I even planned what I was going to specifically eat when I got here, but after awhile I didn't feel so hungry.

I called my dad first, but he didn't answer. I called Lily second because I wanted to let someone know that I had made it safely. I told her where I was staying and what room number I was in. I gave her whatever information one would need to find me in case of an emergency. Lily really gave me a lot of encouragement. She told me that I was very brave for traveling down here by myself to meet Cynthia. She made me feel a lot better about my decision to do this. The queasiness in my stomach made me start to think that this wasn't such a smart idea after all.

I stared at the address until I got brave enough to follow through with the plan. I grabbed my keys, my purse, and headed to the first address.

I pulled up in front of a small, yellow house. I double-checked my piece of paper by matching the numbers on the paper with the numbers written in black on the front steps. That anxious feeling started again in the pit of my stomach as I walked up on the porch and rang the door-bell. I rang it a few times before I heard a soft voice say, "Who is it?"

"Uh... it's... Truly," I said.

"Truly who?" she asked.

"Truly Michaels. Uh, you don't know me," I said.

"Well, why you are ringing my door then?" she asked.

"I'm looking for Cynthia Pratt."

After I said that, she immediately swung open the door, "Why would you come here looking for her? She doesn't live here. She hasn't been by here for months now."

I looked down at the woman. She was short, dark-skinned and had short gray hair. She had on some stretch pants and a t-shirt and some open-toed sandals. She looked like she was on her way out or just getting back.

"I'm sorry for just popping up like this, but this is one of the addresses I had for her so I stopped here first," I explained.

"Who exactly are you, and why are you looking for Cynthia?" she asked.

"I know this sounds crazy, but I am her daughter, and I just found out about her, like, a few days ago. I am looking for her. I want to meet her," I said.

The woman just stood there and looked at me. I didn't know how to feel because it was hard to tell if this lady was mad at me for ringing her door. Or was this just how she treated everyone?

"So, you saying you are Cynthia's baby. What is your name?"

"Truly," I said.

"Oh my goodness, oh my sweet goodness, come on in."

I walked into her house, and it smelled like banana nut bread and coffee. "I was just 'bout to eat me a slice of banana bread and drink some coffee. Would you like some?"

Usually, I would turn food down when people offer because I was too shy, but I hadn't eaten anything since breakfast. That banana bread would sure hit the spot right now. I sat at her dining room table. She brought me a cup of coffee, sat down, and we began to talk.

"How rude of me, I didn't even introduce myself. I am Claire Mae Jones, but you can just call me Mae."

"Nice to meet you Mae," I said.

"So what brings you here? Where are you from? Does Cynthia know you're here?" she said, spurting out questions from left to right.

"Well, to answer your first question, I wanted to meet my mother for the first time. I have come from Kansas and no, Cynthia does not know I am looking for her," I said.

Mae took a sip of her coffee, "What a pleasant surprise."

"So how do you know Cynthia?" I asked. "Why would she be sending letters to my Dad from here?"

"So that's who told you about your mother, your dad?" she asked.

"Yes. He told me everything that he knew about the situation but he couldn't answer my questions about who she is or who my real father is."

"For starters, I'm your grandmother," she said.

My mouth flung open. "Why didn't you tell me? Your kin to me and you ain't even acting like it!" I said.

"Baby, I'm just as surprised as you. Honey, you come popping up on my door step looking for ya Momma, what was I'm supposed to say, 'Give grandma some suga'? I had to wait to the right time to tell ya who I was."

"You're right," I said with a giggle. "So you are Cynthia's mother?"

"No. I'm your Daddy's mother."

Everything was such a shock to me. I learned so much from Mae that day. I learned more than I expected. Mae wouldn't tell me much about my mother. She said that it would be better to wait and ask her the questions face to face. What Mae did talk to me about was my father. I found out that he was in the military and that he died in combat. My mother was pregnant with me when he passed. I found it rather weird that my mother didn't keep me. It is unfortunate that lives are lost in war, and it hurts many families. But why would she give me away?

Mae got out a photo album and showed me pictures of my dad when he was little, when he was in high school, and when he married my mother. Mae pointed to this picture of my dad and another little boy who she said was my Uncle Stephen. She said that my dad had the sweetest smile, but that on this day he got into a lot of trouble. She said that she had taken that picture earlier that day before he had put a betta fish with her goldfish. He had a friend who owned the betta fish. This type can't live with others very well because it would eat the other fish. My dad didn't believe his friend so his friend double-dog dared him to put the fish in the bowl to see if it was true. She said he got a good whipping that day.

Mae continued to flip through the photo album until she reached a picture of my dad in his military uniform. I stared at the unknown man trying to relate to him in any way I could, but nothing.

"What are you feeling right now?" Mae asked.

"Nothing," I said.

"What made you come here young lady? It obviously wasn't because you felt *nothing*."

I continued to stare at the photo, "I feel confused."

"Now that seems more like the truth."

"I don't want to feel this way. I just wish this would have never happened. I wish Pamela would have not been so evil and told me that I was adopted like that. That was really messed up." I hung my head low in disappointment.

Mae grabbed my chin, forcing me to hold my head up, "It is better to be confused than to feel nothing at all. We have to possess a level of vulnerability before we can grow. The vulnerability is when you admit you're confused. If you're never confused about your life then when will you ever go on the journey to answer the questions of life? What's life all about? What's my purpose here on earth? These are the types of questions lots of people ask. But who is bold enough to search for the answer? I think you were pretty bold to come all the way down here."

"You do?" I asked feeling a little brighter.

"Honey, yes! To not acknowledge the pain deep inside is walking in denial. You won't go anywhere denying what is really going on inside of you."

Mae sat quietly looking at me as I pondered on what she just said.

"You know, Mae. I question everyday why I am here. I feel like I am chasing something that isn't meant for me to have. I just want to be loved, accepted. It has just been too hard to get my life together." I started to cry out of frustration.

Mae handed me some tissues. "Truly, everyone on the earth is meant to love and be loved. The key is that you have to have patience for both. You have to first love your Creator, and then learn to love yourself. This must happen before you can love someone else. Show yourself some grace when you make a mistake. You will be loved by another in due time. You must wait on God for the proper time and the proper person."

Mae sent me away feeling really good that we met. At the same time, she multiplied my questions. There were many questions I had that she couldn't answer or refused to. She gave me the last known address she had for Cynthia. I pulled out my yellow sheet of paper to write it down but saw that it was identical to the second address I already had. Mae told me that the second address was of a church my mother attended. She said she didn't know if she still went there, but I could stop by and see. She instructed me not to go by there until Wednesday because there would be no one there to help me. She also told me when I stop there, I should ask for a lady named Terri who she thought was the pastor there. Terri could possibly tell me how to contact my mother.

I was too exhausted for anymore surprises today, so I

decided to go back to my motel room and wait a couple of days to meet my mother on Wednesday.

I didn't sleep very well the next two nights. I had a lot on my mind. I dreamt another dream. This dream was very short. I was standing in a long hallway with doors on both sides.

*There were doors stretched for miles. I starting walking, looking from side to side where I saw different signs on each door that said, "Pick one. Pick me. Which one will you choose?" I was very confused. I didn't know which door was right for me. All of a sudden, I was facing a door in front of me. This door looked much different than the other doors. The sign on this door read, "Do you trust Me?" I reached out and opened the door. At first, it was completely dark inside until a light started shining. A figure came forward from beyond what I could see. It was the most beautiful being I ever saw. It wasn't human because I've never seen human beauty so flawless. I shielded my eyes from the brightness of the light. The being approached me with its arm extended and fist balled. I immediately reached out, already knowing what to do, it dropped a key into my hand. I looked at the key in my hand and there was some very small print. I pulled the key close to my eyes and it said, "Jeremiah 29:11."*

I awoke Wednesday morning pondering this dream. I grabbed the Bible provided by the motel room from the nightstand by my bed. I opened it to Jeremiah 29:11; it read, *"For I know the plans I have for you," says the Lord. "They are plans for good and not for disaster, to give you a future and a hope."* After journaling my dream, I decided to go exercise to work off the stress. Time flew by. I looked up at the clock on the wall, and I realized that I had worked out for over forty-five minutes. It only seemed like fifteen. Before I went to go see my mother, I wanted to spend some time in the presence of the Lord. I hadn't talked to Him in awhile. I felt like He betrayed me. I felt like God put me on this earth with no direction. My whole life I have been living a lie. For twenty-three years I thought that I was my mother's child, my father's daughter. But I was not. I found out that I was really a charity case. Why would my mother leave me? Why would God let her abandon me? She is living it up while I'm an emotional wreck. God has some explaining to do and I was going to get my answer today.

I stomped my way back to my room. I tried to slam the door, but it was one of those retractable doors. I watched as it slowly shut. I began to cry. My anger turned into weeping. My bitterness turned into pity. I felt alone. I wept, asking "Why?" Silence. When my tears stopped flowing, there was peace and stillness in the room. I grabbed my journal, reading over and over again Jeremiah 29:11. "God does have a plan for me. I just have to trust Him."

I sat a little bit longer in the silence. When I got up, I

didn't feel different but now I had more faith. I was ready to face Cynthia.

I showered and grabbed a bite to eat. Lying in my bed now, waiting on time, I stared at the clock with big red numbers on the nightstand. It read 2:57 p.m. In two hours I was instructed by Mae to go to the second address on my list. I lie down until I was ready to leave. I watched the clock tick from 2:57 p.m. to 3:33 p.m. I got myself together and went to my car. I sat there for a bit, waiting until I had enough boldness to stick the key into the ignition and actually go. My stomach was turning. The nervousness in my stomach made me feel like I had to use the bathroom, so I ran back to my room. I was scared! When I got to the door, I forgot all about my nausea because there was one single rose lying on the ground in front of my door. I picked up the rose and looked over both of my shoulders but saw no one. I opened the door with my room key and stepped in.

I was too curious to be afraid. But I did have one concern: Should I start considering this person a stalker and not a secret admirer?

I opened the small card attached to the rose, it read, "It is said that a dozen roses is the way to a woman's heart. Here is the twelfth one." Immediately there was a knock at the door.

I walked slowly to the door and shouted, "Who is it?"

A voice responded, "Mark."

# Eleven

I stood there not sure what to think. I ran to the bathroom to check my hair just to make sure that I wasn't looking messy. I couldn't believe he was on the other side of my door. *Was he my secret admirer the entire time? What is he doing here? How did he know where to find me?* My thoughts were interrupted as he knocked again. I ran and opened the door, "What are you doing here?" I asked.

He said, "I showed up for practice a few days ago and my mother said that you weren't going to be there for a week. I asked her why but she wouldn't tell me. It took a while but she explained everything to me. Don't be mad at her; I made her tell me. She doesn't usually tell people's business. That's why I had to pry it out of her."

Her telling him was the least of my worries. I was just shocked that he was here, in my room, with me!

"So, she told you and you came all the way down here? Why would you do that? And how did you find my room?" I asked.

"Do you mind if I come in?" he asked.

"I'm sorry, yes. You can come in. It's just that I was not expecting anyone. Let alone you."

Mark walked in and looked around. "After I talked with my mother about you leaving, I contacted Vanessa.

She didn't seem to know much about you leaving so she talked to your parents. Your dad called me over, and I got the information from him."

"Please forgive me, but I am very confused right now." I said closing the door behind him, "I have been getting these roses for the past few months. Have you been sending them to me?"

He nodded. "I came to your room today to give you the last one. I was really nervous because I didn't know how you would take me just popping up. 'Cause the last time I popped up you went off."

I covered my face in embarrassment.

He continued, "Earlier I knocked on your door but you weren't here so I left it. I went back to my room. I sat on my bed and talked myself out of doing it. So I came back to get the rose back and it was gone. I just went ahead knocked to talk to you."

"You like me?" I asked.

"Yes, I do. I've been trying to hint to you all this time. I know this is not very professional, and I don't do this with all of my dance associates, though you seem to think that I do."

"What do you mean by that?" I asked.

"Just the fact that you thought my cousin Miranda was my girlfriend… and you thought that I was trying to date your sister… and you thought that I was trying to cheat on my deceased wife with you because of what my four-year-old said."

"All right, I get the picture," I laughed. "Matter-of-fact where is Istas?"

"She is with my parents. She is fine."

"Oh, I know. Your mother is amazing," I said with a smile. "I just can't believe you came all the way down here to support me." I said flopping down onto the bed.

"Truly, you always have your guard up like you are trying to protect yourself from something. Now I understand why you have been like that. Let me tell you something. You can't live this life all on your own. You have to let people help you. That's why I showed up unexpectedly. To catch you with your guard down so you won't reject the support you need right now."

"I don't know what to say. I know I should have something to say but I don't."

"You don't have to always have the answer," he said. "Is it okay if I sit next to you?"

I nodded my head. He took a seat next to me. He continued, "I know that I have taken a big risk by coming out here and not really knowing what your feelings are for me. Like I was saying, my mother told me about you finding out your birth mother was here in Arizona. I care about you Truly, and I didn't feel like this was something you should go through by yourself. So I came here."

I was twirling the rose in my hand thinking about what he said feeling safe, really safe.

We sat in silence for a few moments. "I will only stay

if you want me to," he said softly.

I looked up at him and nodded, "Yes, I would like you to stay." After some time, the conversation lightened up. We started talking about our journey to Arizona. He told me about the woman sitting next to him on the flight he caught here. He said that she keep falling asleep on him. Her head kept nodding to the left and landing onto his shoulder. He eventually stopped pushing her head off. He said that he looked out the window the entire time and pretended that she wasn't drooling on him. He said he managed by studying how many different shapes of clouds there were in the sky. I told him about Derrick and how I had to dance to a country song. Then pay him back by teaching him some ballet steps.

Our conversation turned more serious as I told him about the three addresses that I had for my mother. I explained to him the conversation I had with Mae. Then I told him that it was now time to check out the second place on the list. I was so amazed by his interest in me especially since we've known each other for such a short time.

On our way we stopped at his motel room to grab his wallet and jacket before we headed off to the church. He decided to drive so that I could just relax. It felt so much better having someone there with me. Now all I had to do was meet my mother for the first time.

Mark and I pulled up in front of a small, brick building with one car parked in front. I matched the sign

"The Healer's Temple" and the address with the writing on my sheet of paper. Once we confirmed that the information was accurate, we went inside. The church was lit but there was no one there. It smelled of Pine Sol and bleach as if someone had just cleaned. When we walked into the church, the sanctuary was immediately in front of us. The carpet was a deep red and the benches were a dark brown. The wood creaked as we walked side by side down the aisle calling to see if there was anyone there. We reached the front of the sanctuary. In front of the altar, there were two bouquets of plastic flowers on each side. The wildness of the arrangement drew me close. I walked to my right while I touched each petal as if they were real. I looked over my shoulder and Mark had picked up an old hymn book and was flipping through the pages. For a short while, we both were distracted with the objects of our attention until a soft voice said, "Can I help you?"

"I-I-yes. We are looking for Cynthia Pratt. We were told that we could find her here?" I said.

"You were told by who to come here looking for her?" the woman asked.

"By Mae. Claire Mae. No, first by my dad, Brian, then Claire Mae." I was so nervous I couldn't get my story straight. I couldn't tell if this woman was annoyed with us being here or not.

"And who are you?" she asked.

"I am Truly Michaels. I am Cynthia's daughter. She

put me up for adoption when I was born, and I came here to meet her."

"Does she know you're coming?" the woman asked.

"No, that's just it, she doesn't. No one I know has her number, so I've been stopping at these addresses to see if I could find her." I held up my piece of paper.

"What do you have there?" she asked reaching out for the yellow paper. She took it from my hand, read it, then handed it back. "Do you mind waiting here for a moment?"

We both agreed and took a seat. Mark was still holding the hymn book, but he wasn't looking in it now. We sat silent in the sanctuary until the woman came and invited us to follow her. Not knowing where we were headed, we followed her to a conference room. On the table were bottles of water, a coffee pot, and some refreshments. She invited us to come in and sit down.

"Are you Terri?" I asked.

"Yes, I am," she said.

"Have a seat. I want to introduce myself. I am Pastor Terri Williams. You said that you are Truly. I remember that because that is a very unique name. I don't know any other person with the name Truly. And what is your name young man?" she asked Mark.

"My name is Mark Brown," he said as he stood to shake her hand. *He is such a gentleman*, I thought to myself.

"Feel free to help yourself," she said, pointing to the

refreshments on the table.

Mark grabbed both of us a bottle of water, as I reached for a couple of cookies. The cookies were the vanilla kind with the hard strawberry filling in the middle. They reminded me of the times when I was little. When I was about eight years old, it was this lady who sat next to my family every Sunday at church who would give these cookies to her granddaughter to keep her quiet in the service. I used to gaze lustfully at the cookies while the girl nibbled so quietly. I guess the lady read the look in my eyes because she started bringing enough for her granddaughter and myself.

"So you said that you are the daughter of Cynthia Pratt and you have come here to see her," she said. "I have been pastoring here for about six years now and Cynthia and I have grown close. She has been a member here for about four years. She is very faithful. She heads our praise dance team."

"She dances?" I asked.

"Yes, she does. And she does it beautifully. She definitely has a gift from God. She asked me one day if she could do a dance for the congregation. After that I told her I wanted her to get a group of people together and minister through dance. Ever since that day, she has lead the dance praise team.

"So are you two married?" she asked.

I choked on my water as it went down, "N-no. We are not; just friends," I said.

"Not married yet, huh?" she said, smiling.

We both looked at each other and smiled awkwardly. "We're not dating. We're just friends," he said.

I quickly changed the subject, "So you know Cynthia. When's the last time you talked to her?" I asked.

"Yesterday. We meet once a week, and I know for sure she doesn't know you two are here because she didn't mention anything to me about you."

"Did she ever tell you she had a daughter? Does she speak about me, or am I just a person of her past?"

"I can't tell you exactly what she has told me for confidentiality purposes, but I can tell you that yes, I know about you. And you are not someone she just mentioned once or twice. She does speak of you frequently."

I jumped out of my seat, "I just don't understand! Then why does she pretend that I don't exist? Why does she continue to talk about me to people when she doesn't even want to contact me? She sends my father letters and he sends her pictures of me. Did anyone ever think about how I would feel about all of this?" I was now pacing back and forth.

Pastor Williams watched me pace back and forth for a moment. Then in a gentle voice she replied, "What would you say to her if she were standing right here?"

I stopped pacing and froze. "I would say... I'm lost."

Everyone in the room sat still. I continued, "I would say you hurt me. I would say you left me. I would say you lied." I began to cry.

Pastor Williams got up from her seat and embraced me. I cried in her shoulder. She smelled like vanilla and peppermint. She handed me a tissue, and I sat back in my seat. Mark put his arm around me. She sat back down at her desk.

"I know that your mother has hurt you, that is obvious. The hurt is the thing that we see and feel the most. But I want you to be open to what I am about to say to you. Let's take our eyes off of all the hurt your mother has caused you. Let's think of the good things she has done."

"Good things? She hasn't done any good things!" I said angrily.

"Are you sure about that?" she asked.

"Yes, I'm sure! She hasn't had me for twenty-three years!"

Pastor nodded her head. "Listen closely to what I am about to say. You have just mentioned again the hurt that Cynthia caused. She wasn't there for you. That is the hurtful side of what your mother has done. Now let's talk about the good she has done." My anger began to subside. Once I calmed down, I started thinking about all the good I could think of that my mother has done for me. "One thing I can say is that she had me. She found a safe place for me to go once I was born. I guess that's the best choice she could have made."

"Yes, yes and what else?" She asked.

I sat there for a moment. "She could have given me up

and forgot about me but she kept in touch all these years. Now that I come to think about it, my dad said that he had sent her one of my high school graduation pictures."

"See there is some good about your mother. I'm pretty sure if you sat a little longer you could think about a couple of more good things that would change your mind about her."

I smiled as I used the tissue to wipe my last tear away. I felt the same peace that I felt in my motel room when I was still before the Lord.

"Truly, you must allow your healing to start here. I know that this entire week has been tough emotionally. You have every right to feel the way that you do. But in order to receive your healing, you must forgive your mother. The way we begin to forgive is by not focusing on the hurt that a person has caused us. This is why I wanted you to try and find something good about Cynthia, so that you can start that healing process. There is absolutely no way you can return home with that anger and bitterness in your heart. What if this is the only time that you will be able to meet your mother? Do you really want to let the only time you meet her be in strife? If you don't forgive your mother, and all the others who have hurt you, you are going to grow to be a burdened, old, and bitter woman who has no one around because she has pushed everyone away because of her unforgiving heart."

I stared closely at her. I could tell the seriousness of what she was telling me, "Even if your mom did none of those things you identified or you never get the chance to meet her you still must forgive. The forgiveness is not for her, it's for you."

I nodded in agreement, yet I still had one last question. "I understand the bitterness it takes to have unforgiveness towards someone. I've felt pretty bitter lately. But forgiving her angers me. Its like I am letting her off the hook. I guess I don't understand how forgiveness is for me and not for her," I admitted.

Pastor Williams arose from behind her desk. She pulled her chair closer to where I was sitting. She leaned in and grabbed my hand, "The forgiveness is for you because when you forgive people when they hurt you God will forgive you of your offenses against Him."

I smiled at her knowing she was right. "I know how much I need God's forgiveness." *Well I guess I will be forgiving Pamela,* I thought.

"Now, go meet your mother for the first time and try to recover some of whatever it is that you've missed. And remember, Truly, you are not lost. You are exactly where you are supposed to be."

Before we left Pastor Williams' office, she let us know that she called my mother to tell her we were on our way. She said that it was the right thing to do, to let Cynthia decide if this was what she wanted. I was proud when she said Cynthia was waiting on us. Pastor Williams gave us the exact directions to get to her house. She said it wouldn't take long. She only lived five minutes away.

It was just as she said. Five minutes and we were standing in front of Cynthia's house, matching the numbers on the paper to the numbers on the front of her house. We started walking to the door, and I started giving notice to my emotions. Up until this moment, I felt the emotion of anger. But that emotion was no longer there. I took to heart everything that Pastor Williams spoke to me. Now the emotions I felt were fear and curiosity.

We were half-way up the sidewalk to the front door and the door creaked opened. Mark and I both stopped. The door then opened completely.

"Hello Truly. Hello young man. You can come in." She was obviously expecting us. I wondered if she had ever dreamed of this moment before. The moment she would meet me.

We walked in. We stood awkwardly at the front door like people do when they've never been to someone's house before. Both of our eyes were on her closely.

We were still standing, frozen in place like mannequins as she walked into the living room. She turned around and said, "Here, come, have a seat. I would offer you some refreshments, but I know you just came from the church and she probably stuffed ya' pretty good. Do you want something to drink?"

We both declined. As we were making our way to our seats, she asked for a hug. I turned and embraced her. I smelled the same vanilla perfume that was on Pastor Williams. When we were finished, her face was full of tears. I took a seat on the sofa next to Mark. She sat across from us.

I looked around the living room. Cynthia didn't seem like she had much family or knew many people. She only had a few pictures on the wall and they looked like people who may go to church with her. There was a picture of her and Pastor Williams. I guess they were closer than I thought. I looked behind me. There were pictures of Cynthia dancing. She was beautiful.

"Truly, I don't know what to say. This isn't a surprise for me. I always knew this day would come. It's just a shock to finally see you here."

"How did you know? You always planned on meeting me one day?" I asked.

"In my heart I wanted to meet you, but I could never bring myself to do it. I was embarrassed. Ashamed for what I did. But at that time, I felt it was the right thing to do. The right thing was to allow you to live life with love from a mother and a father. I wanted you to have the life I never had. When your real father died, it devastated me. I got the one thing that I dreaded since I was a little girl," she said.

"What was that?" I asked.

"To be a single mother," she said. "My dad left my

mother and my granddad left her mother. It was a cycle that I just wanted to break. I didn't want to bring a child into the world without having the love of a mother and a father. Brian and Pamela were wonderful. God could not have given me more wonderful people."

"Why do you say God did this?" I asked starting to feel my anger rise again. "I'm pretty sure that he would have rather you to have kept me than give me away like you did."

"Truly, I know you are hurt and you ask me questions that I don't quite have all the answers to. But one answer I can give is that if you can't trust anyone, you can trust God. You have every right to doubt me, but never doubt God."

At that moment, I felt like I didn't need to hear anything else. That day I settled in my heart to love God and believe He loves me back. I felt silenced. I know I should have many questions, comments but my mind was pretty blank at the time. I didn't know if Mark felt the awkwardness of the silence or if he was really interested. Then he chimed in:

"I think Truly is just really emotional and we all can understand why. What I think she really wants is to know who you are. I know that it is not her desire to be rude because she is not like that. It's just that she is going through a lot right now."

"Believe me, I do understand why she may be angry," she began. "I just want to try to do my best at making this time between us as productive as possible. To start with me, the question of 'Who am I?' I am single. I have no other children. I grew up in Wisconsin where my mother is from. I had only one brother. I have no idea where he is now. My mother is deceased and as I told you, my father left when I was very young. My mother did her best. I think the best thing my mother could have given me is dance. She didn't dance, but she encouraged me to do it. She never once doubted my ability to do what I dreamed to do. She worked very hard to see that I could afford every class along with the ballet slippers.

"I moved to Arizona to go to college for dancing. Here's where I met your father, Truly. When I met him I was pretty much a loner. Dance was my love and passion but I eventually fell for him. Your dad was persistent until he got a ring on my finger. We immediately started building a home together. He went away on tour but never came home. I found out shortly after his funeral that I was pregnant with you. I had no job, no home, nothing except to stay with his mother. I did enough to survive. Losing him was difficult for me. It was like I gave up. Every day I fought the tears, but they paralyzed me. I let myself get into a deep depression about my loneliness. I started looking to give you away before you were born.

"That's when I met Brian and Pamela. They couldn't have any more children. I felt peace with giving you to them. They were a perfect fit. I have a lot of regrets in my life. My one major regret is letting the effects of my mistakes dictate my outcome."

I interrupted, "What do you mean letting your mistakes dictate your outcome?"

She breathed in deeply and let out a loud sigh, "If I could take it all back I would have not given you up so easily. I didn't fight. This is what I've lacked, the ability to fight when things get hard. Not fighting led me to living a life less than I believe I was supposed to live." Her face shifted from sadness to frustration. She continued, "I wanted to be a dancer, the greatest dancer of my time. I know I have the gift every time I minister in front of that church.

"I gave dance up like I gave you up after losing your father."

We both were wiping handfuls of tears from our faces until Mark jumped up and grabbed a box of tissues, passing them out.

"I know you are angry with me, I know you are. But you must promise me, Truly that you are not going to let bitterness, nor the mistakes of others, steal your joy and cripple your purpose."

I listened to my mother's story and for once I realized that she was human. I never once considered the pain and hurt she was suffering from. After getting her side of the story, I realized that I didn't have it bad after all; I was really blessed to have Brian and Pamela as my parents because some children in my situation aren't as fortunate as I am.

I stood and hugged my mother. When we embraced, I felt like there was a break in the atmosphere; a break from many years of heaviness off of my mother. To me it seemed like she felt I was finally convinced that she did make the best decision for me at the time. My mother wept; her tears ran harder than a river over a broken ledge. At that moment, I believed my mother was sincerely sorry for the choices she had made. I believed she really made decisions at that time she thought were best for me, and I appreciated her for that. I grabbed a couple of more tissues off a coffee table and handed them to her.

Cynthia excused herself to the bathroom. Mark and I were sitting very closely on the couch. I felt him look over at me. I looked back at him and smiled. I could feel tingly sensation in my body as we locked eyes.

"Truly, I admire you," he said softly.

"You do?" I asked excitedly.

"Yeah. You are so brave coming down here to meet Cynthia. I don't know if I could have done that."

"So you think I'm brave?" I asked.

"Yep." He grabbed my hand and squeezed it.

*I can't believe this is happening,* I thought.

Cynthia returned to the living room opening the window for some fresh air. She went into the kitchen and came back with some refreshments before taking her seat again.

She spoke up first, "So how long are you two here for?"

"Maybe just for one more night. Now that we've met you, there is no other reason for us to stay much longer," I said.

"I understand," Cynthia said nicely.

"So Cynthia, tell me more about yourself," I said.

Mark placed his hand in between us and interrupting the conversation, "Sorry, but I think I should excuse myself to let ya'll get to know each other more privately. Truly I'll go and wait in the car. Cynthia, it was a pleasure meeting you," he said, sticking out his hand.

I watched him walk outside and close the door behind him.

"What a nice young man," Cynthia said. "Are you two dating?"

"No," I said.

"Are you married?" I asked.

"Nope," She said.

"Are you dating?" I asked.

"I've dated a couple of times but nothing ever serious," she replied.

"So what do you do Truly?" she asked.

"Currently, I work at a coffee shop."

"That's it?"

Very offended I asked, "What do you mean, 'that's it?'"

She smiled. "I know you dance. Your dad told me you

do. I was just surprised you didn't mention it. That's what I meant," she explained.

"Oh," I mumbled calming down.

"What do you enjoy about dancing?" she asked.

"The freedom. When I dance I can do whatever I want while on that floor."

She smiled.

"I'm not going to lie. I find it really funny that you dance as well," I said.

"Yes I do. Why don't you come follow me."

Cynthia got up and headed into the kitchen. She opened a door where there was a flight of stairs that lead to a basement. I was a little hesitant but followed her down the stairs.

When I stepped onto the last step it was like walking into the room of a dance studio. There was one wall which had a full length mirror across it. I walked across the floor seeing my smiling reflection. I grabbed a hold of the *barre* running my hand across the length of the bar. I turned around with my back toward the mirror facing Cynthia, "O-M-G! You, like, have your own studio in your house. This is... I can't believe it. So whenever you feel like it you can come downstairs and dance."

"Yes. It took me almost two years to save up the money and build this down here."

I took a spin in the middle of the floor ending with a leap, elevation then another leap.

"I thought you would like it. This is why I brought you down here," Cynthia said.

I was so fascinated with what I saw it was as if no one was even speaking to me. I was in my own world. I walked past her to a wall which hung several trophies, plaques, awards. On the same wall hung costumes, sashes, and tutus, on a clothing rack.

"I wear this when I praise dance," she explained, pulling on a silky white garment. The rest of that stuff I'm just collecting."

"What are these for?" I asked pointing to the plaques on the wall.

"Those were from dance competitions I was in during college."

I picked one up rubbing the dust off of it. "Best Female Solo Performer: Cynthia Pratt."

"Truly, please come have a seat," she said.

I turned around where she had placed two chairs in the center of the floor. We both took a seat.

"This is a beautiful studio you have, Cynthia. Thanks so much for sharing it with me," I said.

"You're very welcome. I just hope showing you this motivates you," she said.

"How so?" I asked.

"This studio is beautiful but it is hidden. It doesn't matter how beautiful or talented someone is if it is hidden. Life has dished you an interesting hand. But I encourage you not to let your beauty and talent stay hidden. Shine. Go forth. Pursue dance like never before. Stop hiding behind that espresso machine. You were created to dance, so dance."

I thanked Cynthia for the encouragement. For about thirty more minutes we stayed in her studio. She showed me pictures of herself and my biological dad when they were younger. It wasn't until we heard Mark walking around upstairs that we left the studio to join him.

Once we got upstairs, Cynthia started preparing dinner for us. She invited us to come to church with her that evening. She was dancing that night and thought that we would enjoy ourselves. She pulled out another album that she kept all of the pictures of me that my dad sent her over the years. There were pictures of Vanessa and I together. Those pictures were the most embarrassing. I couldn't believe how much time passed seeing my younger self.

After we helped Cynthia clean up the dinner dishes we left for church. It felt really great to be introduced to Cynthia's church members as her daughter. Some nodded and welcomed Mark and I, but most of them said, "I didn't know you had a daughter."

The part of the service came for Cynthia to dance. Three other women joined her in the front, but the only one I could keep my eyes on was my mother. They danced a wonderful praise dance. As Cynthia danced, I couldn't believe the similarity that we shared; she danced, I danced. When she finished, I stood to give her a standing ovation. I looked at her as she took a bow and thought, "I wonder if I am going to look like her when I get older?"

After service was over we stood in the background as I watched Cynthia mingle with the other church members. We waited to say goodbye. Once everyone cleared out Cynthia and Pastor Williams approached us.

Cynthia thanked us for coming. We thanked her for having us. I leaned in to give her one last hug before leaving the church. I whispered in her ear and said, "Mom, I forgive you."

I felt her embrace tighten before she let me go.

Pastor Williams began to speak: "Wow, Truly. You have a great responsibility ahead of you. There are some things that you must do and some time that will pass before you take on this responsibility. A lot of the tension in your family is going to cease. You are going to be blessed with great responsibility for others. You will feel overwhelmed at first because you are going to think 'I'm so young.' But know that the Lord will never put on you more than you can bear. You are going to be able to take on everything that you are given because you were created for a purpose that only you can fulfill. Keep the young man you brought today close by you."

I worshipped God in my heart. Everyone there was very supportive. I felt surrounded by people who loved, appreciated and believed in me. Though Cynthia and I just met that day, I believed she believed everything that she told me. She believed that I could do it. That day she had a special place in my heart.

Mark and I returned to our motel rooms. We agreed that we would meet up in the morning for breakfast to discuss our journey back to Kansas. That night I slept like a baby: sweet and peaceful.

# Twelve

I woke up the next morning, anticipating the invitation I received from Mark the night before to have breakfast. After starting the day with a workout, I sat waiting in the restaurant located right outside of the motel. The diner was very small, looking as if it could fit no more than fifty people at a time. I sipped on the water the waitress started me off with as I sat waiting for Mark to arrive at the restaurant. I pulled out my cell phone to check the time. I saw that there were three missed calls and a voicemail. Two missed calls were from my father and the third was from Casey. I watched Mark walk through the door as the hostess pointed him back to the table where I was seated.

"I ordered you a glass of orange juice and water," I said, as I pushed the two glasses closer to his side of the table.

I stared at him out of nervousness and curiosity. I was so nervous because this was the first time I had to be with him alone, on purpose. I was curious because this was the first time that I actually got a good look at who he was, but realizing I didn't know him.

He looked up at me. His head was slightly bent into his orange juice glass as his eyes popped out of his sockets as he tried to drink and ask me a question. He managed to squeeze out a "What?"

I laughed, "It's just, I realize that I don't even know you. And now we are here in this strange place together. So unexplainable."

The waitress butted in before he could answer. She took both of our orders and let us know our food would be out shortly.

He looked at me, and I stayed quiet to signal that I wanted and needed to hear from him.

"I don't know how to answer that other than to tell you more about myself. Anything you want to know. But to be honest, with you, I asked myself 'Why am I here?' as I was falling asleep last night."

"Well, why are you here? You regret coming?"

"No, absolutely not," he said, grabbing my forearm. "I am enjoying every minute of supporting you because I want you to know that you are not alone. I-I guess the scary, or uncomfortable, rather, question is, why did I feel so drawn to be here? When my mother explained why you came, it was an immediate draw to be here, to follow you. I'm still trying to understand it all."

"And the roses?" I asked.

"Truly, I'm not gonna lie, but you thought so hard that I was feeling your sister that there was no way I could have really let you know it was you I'm interested in. I didn't want you to lose sight of me, so I sent those secret messages, so when you would eventually find out, half the work was already done."

He confidently picked up his cup of orange juice and started drinking out of it. This time making slurping sounds.

"Lose sight?" I laughed. "You sound really sure of yourself. What makes you think I was digging you at all?"

"Mall. Dressing room. Running back and forth checking on me. Get my drift? End of story."

My mouth flung open as if I were waiting for something to be tossed in there as I watched Mark take his plate from the waitress and point to his cup for more orange juice.

He started eating, then looked up at me and said, "I'm just saying."

We finished up our food and Mark had the idea that we should do one more thing before we left. Mark decided to do something relaxing. So we went back to his motel room. I was lying in the bed, watching him lie on the couch across the room. He slept for like two hours, snoring the entire time. I think I may have seen him stir one time and that was to flip from one side of the couch to the other. I guess that was his idea of relaxing.

As for me, I didn't sleep. I was tired a little bit, but just couldn't quiet the thoughts in my mind. The good thing, though, is that I felt safe, really content and safe.

After Mark woke up we went to a nearby restaurant and ate dinner. Because we weren't familiar with Arizona, he decided that we should just walk the surrounding neighborhood of the motel. As we ventured we came upon a walkway lit by very dim lights. It was so romantic, but I felt very embarrassed feeling the way that I did. We talked but some of the time the quiet breeze of the night was louder than we were. The moment was so comforting.

I looked at Mark out of the corner of my eye and saw that he was looking at me. I turned and said "What?" with a soft giggle.

"What are you thinking about?" he asked softly.

"I don't know," I said.

"You got to be thinking something."

"Okay what are you thinking then?" I said, nudging him.

"I'm thinking about my little girl. I haven't been away from her this long before. I called her but today she was busy shopping with Grandma for a new toy, so she only was semi-focused, but I know she misses me."

We both stared ahead.

"So, Truly, how do you feel about me, really?"

"I mean, I like you. But sometimes I don't know how to feel around you. My heart races when I see you. I tell myself to get it together, especially for the sake of the show. I don't want my emotions getting in the way of our performance together, meaning you, Vanessa, and me."

"You know, I've wondered what's up between you and

your sister. You two just seem not to vibe very well."

I looked at him dead in the eye for the first time the entire night and said, "It's a l-o-o-o-ng story."

Satisfied with that answer he said, "Well, Truly, I'm very interested in getting to know you better, you know on a different level than just friends. We are friends, right?"

I giggled, "Yeah, you have been quiet, I guess, with how you feel."

"I didn't want to come off too strong and like I was desperate. I can't stand females who do that. It's a big turn off. I'm a guy. I wanted to see where you stood so that I wouldn't be too embarrassed. You know I have to see you again, especially until we finish this show."

I just smiled.

"Why are you so quiet this evening? Usually you be talking my ear off, non-stop talking."

"I do not!" I shouted playfully.

"There you go," he said, "that got her talking."

We both laughed until it got silent again.

As we walked down the dimly lit walkway I realized we were crossing over a bridge with a small brook under it. I guess he noticed also as he stopped to stare at the water. I watched as he jumped onto the railing of the bridge and walk across it. When he finished on one side he jumped onto the other railing on the opposite side. It looked really fun to me so I decided to walk across the railing too. I was doing well as I balanced myself by holding my arms straight out in the air.

"So, Truly when do you want to get married?" Mark asked.

I turned to answer him, slipping and falling into the brook. I was fighting the water trying to stay afloat.

Immediately Mark jumped in after me. When Mark made it to me he yelled over my splashing, "Truly! You have to stop kicking and flapping your arms so I can pull you out."

Once he said that I stopped. The water wasn't even that deep.

We both started cracking up.

"Truly what are you doing?" he asked.

"I was just trying to do what you did, then I fell," I explained.

"You were swingin' like you were about to drown. I was trying to help you at the same time tryin' not to get smacked in the face."

We laughed some more as I let him help me out of the water. We made our way back to our motel rooms. After showering and getting a snack and drinks from the vending machine, we went back to my room and talked until I fell asleep. I awoke about 2:00 a.m. when I found myself alone in my room. I picked up my phone where I had a text message from Mark at 1:27 a.m. that read, "Sweet dreams. See you in the morning."

The next morning we got up early, headed for Kansas. The drive back was much more enduring. I had accomplished my goal, and meeting my mother turned out to be great. I had someone to talk to on the way home and share some of the driving responsibility with. The one major thing that kept repeating in my head was Terri's advice to remember to forgive Pamela. All I could think of was what was going to happen next.

# Thirteen

Mark went after Vanessa as she tried to escape him. Her love was so important to him that he was willing to accept her constant rebuke until she gave into his desire to love her. Eventually she did give in. He pulled her close and their faces touched, looking into his eyes; they embraced.

"Did you get that, Truly? Before we embrace, I want you to pull away. But I think, what I am going to add is a lift at this part. Yeah, that's what I am going to do."

Mark walked back and forth as he thought out loud to himself. "Okay, so both of you, as you pull away from me I am going to pull you back. Walk away with your right arm stretched. I am going to grab your wrist and squat down. Here is where we will do the Romeo and Juliet lift. This part needs to be very intimate. Then we will finish with the same ending. Come on Truly, let me practice with you first."

November crept its way in as we finished preparing for the winter recital. We were practicing more often now that the recital was next month.

Dancing with Mark was different ever since we came back from out of town. Sharing that time with him in Arizona made me crush on him even heavier. But he has been different since we've gotten home. He has seemed to become more distant and very focused on this recital. I was very confused. Every time I come around him, the moment is a bittersweet one. Bitter because I have all these emotions that I don't know what to do with. Bitter because he has not made one romantic look, gesture, comment; nothing since we returned. *Did he lead me on?* I thought to myself as he took my hand. My bitterness soon changed to sweetness as he embraced me.

I pulled away, he pulled me near, dropped down to one knee and lifted me. I imagined myself for a quick second as Juliet proclaiming my love for my Romeo. Unlike Juliet, boldly shouting her love from her balcony, I was silently screaming inside. He put me down, arose from the ground, we looked in each other's eyes; it ended.

"Whoa, if I didn't know any better I would say you two were really in love. That was amazing." The gentleman started clapping loudly.

We both stopped and turned to see who this gentleman was. I realized I had seen him before. He was the one who met with Lily a few months ago, inquiring about the director position for the company once Lily steps down.

I quickly pulled from Mark's embrace, a little embarrassed.

"Is this who you will be dancing with in the winter recital?" he asked.

"This is Brett Landers, possibly the new director of

the company," Lily continued. "This is Truly. She is our understudy. Her sister Vanessa will be the leading lady." Vanessa stood up from sitting cross-legged on the ground and shook Brett's hand.

To hear the words, "Truly is the understudy," used to bring up so many emotions, especially anger and a little bit of jealousy, but now something was different. I waited to feel the beat of my heart quicken and my chest tighten as if I were getting ready to suffocate but nothing happened. I stood still, silently knowing that the success of a stranger, the evil intent of a loved one, nor my past, determines my worth and future. I have Cynthia to thank for that lesson.

Brett extended his hand, which I shook, smiling. He seemed so happy to be in this moment with us. I was sure he was certainly Lily's choice to direct the company. At least that's what I sensed as I watched Lily watch him with an approving smile on her face.

I took a seat on the floor in the back of the room as practice resumed. Lily and Brett left and I watched Vanessa and Mark execute the Romeo and Juliet lift. Once it was done to Mark's liking, practiced ended. He grabbed his gym bag and waved "goodbye" to us as he headed out the door.

I began to gather my things into my gym bag. I slipped on a pair of sweats over my stretch pants. Vanessa walked over to me.

"Do you have a little bit of time? Can we talk?"

"Sure."

We both walked over to two chairs in the back of the room and sat down.

"Dad told me about your trip to see your mother. How was that?"

"It was a lot of things: scary, sad, happy, fearful, confirming."

"I bet it was," she said.

"I hope you don't think this apology is too late. The reason why I waited is because I know you have been through a lot in these last few months, so I was just waiting for the perfect time to apologize."

"But you already did that one day at breakfast," I said.

"No. That was *Dad* telling me to apologize. I only feel that it is right for me to apologize to you because *I* am the one who is really sorry. I think I just got caught up in this selfish game where I made everything about myself. I feel like growing up, everything has been about me and what I wanted. The moment the attention got off of me, I acted really childish and evil."

She sat quietly for a moment.

"Another thing I've realized is that I need to be my own person and not let others think for me."

"What do you mean?" I asked.

"I am going to move out soon."

"What! Pamela and Dad are not going to let you do that."

"See Truly, that is the problem. I am twenty-five, going on twenty-six. I have my own career, why not?"

"I guess you're right," I said.

"I know Mom and Dad love us and want the best for us, but one day we have to grow up and make our own decisions. And this is what I want to do." Vanessa stared at the ground. This was the first time in a long time I saw Vanessa's vulnerable side. She looked very humbled.

Lifting her head, looking into my eyes, she said, "You know Truly...I-I didn't know you were adopted either."

I didn't say anything. I just stared back at her.

Vanessa continued, "When Mom told you...when Mom told you were adopted..." I could tell she was confused. She brushed her hand across her forehand, struggling to wrap her mind around the whole ordeal. "I was just as shocked as you were. After you left, Mom and Dad came to my room and told me everything. Then Dad left. I never saw Dad so emotionally wrecked like that ever, especially after you left. He really loves you Truly."

"I know," I said.

"Mom loves you, too."

I didn't respond.

"I know it's hard to believe, but she does."

Pamela and my father started attending marriage counseling. They have seemed to be doing better. At our family meeting, everyone apologized to me for the way they revealed to me I was adopted, but living back home was not the same. For the first couple of weeks on my way to my room, I bypassed looking at any of our family photos hanging on the wall by the staircase. Just recently, I was able to stop and look at my young self. I noticed how naïve I was back then, smiling as if I belonged.

Since Vanessa and I had our heart-to-heart I rarely saw her outside of practice because her modeling had her traveling for shows and photo shoots. My conversations with Pamela were very generic. We only talked about trivial things like, "How was your day?" and "Add what you want on the grocery list because I'm going to the store."

Pamela never spoke again of me being adopted.

My father wanted us to attend family counseling, but I declined. I told him I was not ready to talk about our problems and if I could make an assumption I would say Pamela probably wasn't ready either.

I woke up this morning with nothing on my schedule to do. So I called Lily to see when the studio would be free for me to practice alone. About 4:00 p.m. I was at the studio standing on the dance floor. I brought a new pair of pointe shoes. I really want to grow in my experience as I dancer. I put my pink pointe shoes on and moved around the dance floor stretching and doing whatever movement I could to break them. I stood in front of the mirror; ready to teach myself to pointe dance. I lifted my body to stand as tall as I could as I shifted my body weight to the tip of my toes before losing my balance. As I recovered from stumbling I felt someone walk in behind me. I turned around. It was Pamela.

"Hey Truly, are you busy?" she asked.

"No… not really." I was confused by her presence.

She then pulled up a chair that was up against the wall and took a seat. I turned my back to her to start practicing again. Turning back around I asked, "Is there something I did?"

"Oh no, no. I've just come to talk to you."

I turned completely around to give her my full attention.

"Truly, please grab a seat."

I did as she asked. I sat awkwardly on the side of her. She began to speak. "As you obviously know our family is really recovering from some trying circumstances we have encountered in these past few months."

I sat silent.

"What I came here to do was to apologize to you for the way I have been treating you. Also for the way I told you that you were adopted."

I stared her straight in the eyes, still silent but feeling heated on the inside. I could feel my leg shaking from irritation replaying that day in my mind.

She continued, "Now I know there is absolutely nothing I can do to take back anything that I have done. All I can say today is that I am here to work on our relationship. My first goal was to ask for your forgiveness."

"Why would you do me like that?" I asked. "What have I ever done to you?"

"You've done nothing." She stood up. "That's why your dad and I are in counseling. I need to figure out what's going on in here," she said pointing to her heart.

Seeing her in distress and really trying to apologize, I began to calm down.

"Pamela, I may not be your birth daughter but I do ask for your respect."

"And that you will get from now on," she said.

"Thank you. I forgive you," I said.

After sealing our conversation with a hug I asked her if it was okay if I continued to practice.

She said, "yes" taking her seat again. She watched me practice for a few moments. "Teach me how to do that one thing when you make your feet go out."

"Huh? Are you talking about this?" I motioned by kicking my feet in and out.

"No. You held on to that bar over there."

"The *barre*," I said grabbing a hold of it.

"Yes."

"Oh are you talking about when I did the *rond de jambe*?"

"I guess," she said shrugging her shoulders.

We practiced for about fifteen minutes. I tried to teach her the basics but she kept wanting me to teach her advanced stuff. When she finally gave up on her first ballet lesson, she told me she didn't understand how Vanessa and I moved our bodies like that. "I'm gonna just stick to selling makeup," she said.

I went into Lily's office and let her know we were done. She and Pamela talked for a brief moment before we got into our cars and went home for dinner. Later that night before going to bed I wrote in my journal, "I've forgiven her. God has forgiven me."

The next day I brought in a stack of flyers to work advertising the recital.

Jeremy said I could, as a payback for him not being able to make it. I stayed on my coworkers to make sure a flyer was handed to everyone when they picked up their coffee. People seemed to be more receptive to the idea of supporting the recital knowing it was for a good cause.

I was on the register when my father walked in. He ordered a black coffee and the barista handed him a flyer, "Oh Shelby, you don't have to give him one, he knows about it already. He's my dad."

Shelby went to take the flyer back when my Dad said, "No, it's okay, I'll take this and post it to our student activities board at the college."

"Dad, what are you doing here?" I asked, escorting him to a two top.

"Well, I wanted this coffee, and to tell you I ran into Mrs. Toby, Steven's mother, yesterday."

"Steven?" I said, not too sure of who my father was

talking about.

"His mother, Mrs. Toby, recognized me last night at the grocery store. Steven is a young man you became friends with at school when we first moved here. He came over a couple of times to hang out when you two were younger. And you two used to have those dancing competitions in the living room. But then her family moved because Robert, his dad, is in the military."

"Oh yeah, Steven! So his mother recognized you?" I asked.

"Yeah, funny thing. She said that Steven lives out of state and works for a company where he travels a lot. He is in town now for fall break. He just finished a show early this November."

"That's nice. Sounds like he's doing pretty well."

My dad took a sip of his coffee, "Yeah, it does. But I thought it would be good for you two to catch up, so I invited Mrs. Toby and her family over for dinner this weekend."

"You did? Okay. What day?"

"I figured it could be Friday night because I know you'll be home this Friday. Unless you have something planned?" he asked.

"No I don't," I said. "Dad, thanks for stopping in to see me. I will be home later."

As I got up to go back to work, my dad grabbed my hand, "What is wrong?"

"What do you mean?" I asked.

"Sit down. Now, I know you, Truly. What's wrong? You seem to be very uncomfortable with me inviting the Toby's over. Why?"

"Dad, you know, I don't really want to talk about it. At least not right now. I'm at work."

"I understand, but if you want me to cancel I will," he said.

"No, no, no. Absolutely not. I'm fine. Everything is fine." I bent over and gave him a kiss. "I'll see you later tonight."

I went back behind the counter and started taking drink orders, pretending that I didn't see the look of a concerned father as he left the coffee shop.

I lied. I didn't want to meet the Toby's. I didn't want to hear all the great things Steven was doing. My fear was that everyone would then turn to me wanting to know the great things I was doing, and I will say, "I work at a coffee shop."

I got off around seven o' clock, so I headed to the studio to see if I could catch Lily before she left. I just felt so overwhelmed. I needed to talk to someone, immediately. I was so frustrated with my life and feeling like it was going nowhere. I felt like she was the only one I could truly trust with this insecurity. I pulled up in front of the building, "The light is on. Good, she's still here." I hurried inside, bursting in the door. As I shuffled back to the office I threw open the door and Mark flung around in the office chair.

"Where's your Mom?" I asked.

"She's already gone for the night, what's wrong?" he asked.

"Nothing, I just wanted to talk to her about something but it looks like I'm too late," I said, pushing away the stream of uncontrollable tears that were flowing.

I turned to walk out the door and he followed after me.

"Truly, wait, what's wrong? Give me a chance, maybe I can help."

I whirled around angrily, "You can't help because you're a part of the problem."

I got into my car and sped off.

The night came of the dinner at our house with the Toby's. The formal dining room table was set for eight. Pamela was so giddy, bouncing around the house assigning tasks to everyone. Her anxiousness of having guests over made her stand over my dad and I like a drill sergeant as we were doing what she told us to do. My dad finally got her to sit down in the recliner with a cup of hot tea to relax. I laughed and joked with my father, but inside I wanted to stay hidden away in my room. I only came down because I didn't want anyone to know I was struggling.

7:30 p.m. came around and our dinner guests arrived. Everyone was there except Vanessa, who was always running late due to her other obligations. Dinner was running smoothly as the Toby's talked about their family. Pamela sat quietly as Dad brought up some stuff that happened when Steven and I used to be best friends. We laughed at the funny stories my dad told, but I realized how much people change. I stared at Steven, who used to be my best friend, as everyone talked about the past, but we could barely look each other in the eye. It was very awkward as I looked at him stir the cold mashed potatoes on his plate.

Vanessa walked in and apologized for being late. She sat in the open chair between Dad and Pamela. I watched as Pamela began serving Vanessa, even getting up to refresh the ice tea pitcher because the ice had melted after sitting on the table for an hour. Mr. Toby and my Dad ended up engaging in a private conversation. Mrs. Toby addressed Vanessa, "So you're mother told me a little about all the things you're doing, young lady."

"Yeah, my mother is always running her mouth," Vanessa joked.

"She said I said 'a little,'" Pamela said. "She's just shy. Let me show you some pictures of some of her work."

"No, Momma!" Vanessa said, as Pamela went to the cabinet where she kept all our photo albums. Everyone passed around the photo book. Steven even made his first comment of the night without someone having to invite him to chat.

"Yes, aren't these beautiful? She really has a promising career as long as she stays focused," Pamela explained.

When everyone sat down Mr. Toby looked at me and said, "So Truly, what is it that you do?"

I looked at everyone, waiting for a response, as all eyes were on me, "Um, well I work at a coffee shop in Midtown, and I'm trying to get back into dancing right now. I am actually preparing for a dance recital coming up in about a month."

"Truly is actually Vanessa's understudy. They both are preparing to dance for a charity winter recital being put on by a local dance studio," Pamela said.

"Oh, so you both dance. Wow, Vanessa, you do everything," Mrs. Toby added.

"She is a talented girl... like I said, she is going places," Pamela added.

I waited as the conversation shifted from several different topics to make sure that when I got up from the table it wouldn't be so obvious that I was embarrassed. I grabbed a few plates off of the table and took them into the kitchen. Everyone else migrated into the living room except Steven. My head was stuck in the fridge. He walked over to the sink placing his dinner dishes there. I grabbed a strawberry cheesecake from the fridge.

I got two small plates, "You want some cheesecake?" I asked.

"Yeah I'll take a piece," he said.

I handed him his cheesecake then cut a piece for myself. We were both standing there eating when he said,

"Hello. My name is Steven." He stuck his hand out for a shake.

I playfully slapped his hand away, "Steven what are you talking about?"

"This is good," he said with a mouthful. "I noticed how uncomfortable you have been tonight especially when your mother started to talk about your sister."

"How do you figure that?" I asked.

"I'm good at reading body language," he explained.

"So what is my body language saying now?" I asked.

He cocked his head to the left then to the right as if reading me. "From the looks of it you are thinking, *if this guy doesn't get away from me I'm gonna smack the crap out of him.*"

"Ah, you're wrong. I wouldn't do that. I'm a nice young lady," I said.

"So I was wrong about now, but you didn't say I was wrong about how you were feeling tonight."

I shrugged my shoulders indifferent to what he was saying. I didn't deny or agree. I just pled the fifth.

Seeming to get the message he switched subjects, "Honestly, Truly, I wanted to come in and get to know you. Hearing all these stories our parents were telling when we were younger. At some point we were supposedly best friends."

"I know. I only can remember a little bit too." I stuck my hand out. "I am Truly."

He shook my hand. I continued, "Unfortunately there

is nothing more to tell you than what you heard at dinner. I am a barista and my sister's understudy for the winter recital."

Pamela and Mrs. Toby came into the kitchen, "They already started on the cheesecake. Truly pass me the knife," Pamela said.

Pamela and Mrs. Toby started on their pieces of cheesecake having their own conversation when Steven asked me if I would like to talk outside on the front porch. I agreed and we made our way out. I sat down first on the porch swing. Steven sat on the opposite side pushing the swing back with his legs. I pulled out my cell and started playing a game.

Steven spoke first, "So before our moms interrupted, you started telling me about yourself."

"I pretty much told you all there was to tell," I said.

"No you didn't," he said.

"Yes I did. How are you going to tell me?" I asked starting to get a little annoyed.

"You didn't say nothin' about your hopes, dreams, future; nothin'."

I stopped looking at my phone giving him my full attention. "Wow, okay. I want to eventually move from home and go to school to study dance. Hopefully all that will turn into me becoming an accomplished ballerina. Then I want to open up my own company to train others," I said.

"Now that's a dream." he smiled.

"Thanks."

"In this short amount of time Truly, you really seem to come off as if you are insignificant."

I quietly listened. If I hadn't learned anything else through this journey, I can say I've learned to listen to people.

He continued, "Dreams are looking toward the future. Presently you may be a barista, your sister's understudy but not forever if you don't choose to be. See, if you stay mentally defeated, you will always be those things even though those positions were only for meant for a season."

"Steven that was really cool. Thank you for that. You know people just have been giving me so much wisdom lately. Its like God is talking to me through almost everyone I meet."

"It sounds like God has to keep repeating Himself 'cause someone's not listening."

We both laughed.

"Take me, for example. This is not to brag. I know the passion you have for dancing; I have it too, but I didn't get to my career without hoping, dreaming, praying, wishing. I would have stopped doing those things then I would have no motivation to get to my dreams. Without hope, dreams are non-existent."

"You're so right." All I could do was nod my head in agreement. "Speaking of dreams I really want to become an *en pointe* dancer." I jumped off of the swing to show him what I've practiced so far.

I stumbled a few times before Steven got up and *en pointe* like a pro.

"Whoa! Teach me, teach me!" I exclaimed.

Steven walked me through the proper techniques of *en point* dancing. He also told me not to do it often without my *en pointe* shoes. We exchanged numbers agreeing we would hang out sometime before he left to go home. The Toby's and my parents joined the two of us on the porch as everyone said their good-byes. I joined my family back inside to start cleaning up the dinner dishes. I didn't want to do that. I just didn't feel like helping, so I snuck quietly back to the front porch. I went down to my car, and the door was unlocked, so I grabbed the little jacket that was in the passenger seat and went for a walk. I had no real place to go on this quiet, November night. The cool breeze was very relaxing and the sway of the trees let me know that I could find peace somewhere even if it wasn't in my own home. Looking up into the night sky, I felt this sudden boldness rise up in me.

"God, if you can give purpose to those stars, then surely you have given me purpose."

I walked over to a slim tree planted by the side of the road, shaking the tree at it's bark, "If you can give purpose to this tree than why wouldn't I have purpose?"

The boldness changed to a burst of joy. I continued up the street and a stray dog was coming towards me. I pointed at it, "You have purpose and so do I!" before it turned and ran the other direction.

I ran from one thing to the next, "If you have purpose, then so do I!"

I continued several blocks around my neighborhood. As I was circling back around, I was approaching a house where a man was seated on his front porch. As I approached he shouted, "It's kinda late for you to be walking around, ain't it? It's almost ten o' clock. You know this is a pretty safe neighborhood, but still, things can happen anywhere, right?"

"You're right, but I'm headed back home now," I said.

"Is everything okay?"

"Yes, why do you ask?"

"I don't know, just being a nosy neighbor," he joked.

I laughed and stood there for a moment, not really knowing what to say, when the man's front door opened behind him. It was his teenage son telling him that his wife wanted him. After telling him he would be there in a minute he said, "I usually take a late night walk when I have a lot on my chest." He walked towards me, "I know you don't know me but we're neighbors right? If you have something you need to get off of your chest, I'm all ears."

"Oh no, no, I'm fine," I said.

"I don't know how long you've been going through whatever it is, but I want to encourage you that it's almost over. And when it is, you will see blessings that you never saw coming, and they will all flood you at once. Don't worry about having to tell anyone your problems because they're already taken care of. You just believe in God."

I felt my eyes lift from the sockets in amazement. I smiled and thanked him as I continued toward my house. I felt him staring as I walked away before making his way into his house.

It may have not seemed to my neighbor that his words impacted me as I walked silently away, but they did. After I got home I took my journal out and recorded everything he said. I put on my pajamas and pulled back the covers, craving to finally sleep after this long day, when my phone began to sing. I picked it up and it was a text message from Steven. It read *I really liked talking to you tonight. Do you wanna hang out tomorrow?*

I texted him back to pick me up tomorrow after work at the coffee shop.

Ever since my talk with my sister about making decisions, I thought a few times that taking that trip to Arizona to meet Cynthia was the most sporadic decision I have made in my life. But then, I checked my voicemail message and I heard this angry voice, "So Jeremy told me you put in your two weeks' notice because you were moving to Arizona, and you didn't even tell me first!" Casey's message ended. Here is when I realized my decision to quit my job and move to Arizona to start a new life won the title for the "most sporadic event in Truly's life," by far.

I closed my eyes and quieted my mind for some sleep.

The next day, Steven picked me up after a busy early morning shift at work. I was looking forward to some relaxing and uplifting conversation. Steven's plan that afternoon was for us to go to the museum then get some lunch. We were riding to the museum. He was watching the road, I was watching him. *He is kind of handsome.* I examined him from head to toe. I really liked what I saw.

We went into the museum. He educated me on some of the pieces he knew about. He explained to me that when he was in school he studied dance and art. He said if he didn't love dance so much he would become an art professor.

We walked into the ancient exhibit of the museum. I ran into this figure that had no head. Steven drifted off to another section of the museum. I looked at the sculpture that towered above me. Inside I began to relate to this stony, headless sculpture.

Steven returned, "You must really be fascinated with this. You haven't moved since we came into this section," he said.

I stared at it some more then said, "I'm fascinated by this sculpture because he has no face."

"Okay," Steven chuckled. "He is pretty headless."

"Yes but he's still important," I said.

"Yes... but not really sure where you going with this,"

he said.

"People know you by your face right?" I asked.

He nodded.

"But he has no face, yet he is still in this museum. He is still an important fact of history without his head. I've felt like I wasn't important because people don't know who I am. 'Cause I haven't established myself yet; like I don't have a face. But I don't have to have a *face* to be important." Pointing to the statue, "His entire head is gone yet he is important. I *will* pursue my dreams no matter how small I may be in this large world," I declared.

Steven gave me a slight corner smile, grabbed my hand softly and lead me through the rest of the museum.

# Fourteen

December finally came around and the recital was only two weeks away. Everyone shuffled around making sure costumes were all ordered and assigned to the correct people. All the dance acts were coming together, from the children to the adult group dances. The program was finalized for the night and the *paus de deux* was scheduled as the final dance of the night. I saw Brett with Lily as they went back and forth from the studio to the auditorium. Lily sent all of us emails, letting us know that our final practice would take place the weekend before the recital and we would be required to rest for the remainder of the week. Vanessa and Mark were to practice on Friday night, and he and I would practice Saturday at the auditorium.

All week, I purposed to do stuff that I liked to do. Since I no longer was going to be working as a barista in two weeks, I went from being on the schedule all week to a few days this week and only one day the week of the recital. One of those days, after work, Casey and I went to dinner, and I was able to explain why I made such an abrupt decision. I apologized to her for not telling her in advance. She was stubborn and didn't want to forgive me until after I offered to pay for her food. That fixed it.

Saturday came and I walked into the auditorium. When I arrived, there were people hustling around working on the lighting and the sound. I even saw a few people polishing some beautiful, Greek-inspired pieces of art located around the auditorium. I stood at the back of the auditorium and gazed at the large stage. Imagining myself dancing solo with a thousand pair of eyes looking at me, I tried to guess how many people the auditorium could possibly sit. As I daydreamed, Mark walked onto the stage. He was directing someone to something, pointing toward the ceiling where the lights were. I immediately snapped back to reality and started walking toward the stage.

"Hello Truly! It's beautiful in here isn't it?" With a smile I nodded in agreement.

He continued, "It's so amazing how much God has blessed this event. When we started this, several years ago, it was very small. Then over time, the cause of this has just spread and people come out to support the community. I am so excited to be a part of this."

"Yeah, it is amazing, and to do it in the name of your late wife makes it even more special," I agreed.

He paused in mid-sentence, staring off into space for a moment, "Yeah, you're right." After coming to, he said, "Let's get started."

We practiced and practiced. I went in there with the mindset of business, but the battle between my intentions and emotions warred the entire time we practiced. I hated being that close to him. I got a glimpse of his face from time to time as he focused on every step, his expression reinforced the thought that this was a business arrangement.

We wrapped up practicing, both heading outside, I started walking towards my car.

"Truly, do you mind if I take you to dinner tonight?" he asked.

"I better not, this has been a very long day for me."

"You and I haven't really had a chance to talk since that last big blow up, and I really planned on you saying yes to dinner tonight." He opened the passenger side door, inviting me to get in.

"I'm flattered, but what do you mean when you say 'I really planned on you saying yes to dinner tonight?'" I asked.

He shrugged his shoulder, "I don't know, just what I said. I've been thinking about you, and thought when we meet there will be no other distractions around, just you and I."

Smiling inside, I got into his car. He pulled up to this Mexican restaurant, "I hope you're feeling some burritos tonight."

I didn't care what we ate, I was just happy to be in the presence of someone who "planned to have me around."

I watched as he always did, scarf down his food. He ate this full-size burrito with a side of Spanish rice and beans like there was no tomorrow. He took a sip of his drink and asked, "Do you like your taco salad?" I nodded, my mouth full of food.

"Truly, I have not been able to stop thinking about how upset you were with me that day when you said, 'I was a part of the problem.' What exactly did you mean?" he asked.

"I-I am very embarrassed that I let my emotions get the best of me. So first off, I want to say that I am sorry."

"Forgiven," he said.

"It's just that we had this moment of sharing our feelings toward one another in Arizona. After that there was not much talk about it again. I felt like when you came around me you were different, like you regretted ever sharing your feelings."

He continued to listen to me, "I have liked you since the day I met you. Well, no, I was crushing on you, but then I really started liking you when I saw how much you supported me. I feel like you have been one person who I can be vulnerable around. You knowing my personal story and being there when I met my mother for the first time drew me closer to you. I hope I don't sound crazy, but it has been very difficult to shake these feelings that I have for you."

I waited a few seconds as he stared me straight in the eye. He finally responded, "Truly, you know why you struggle so much emotionally?" he asked.

"What, excuse me? I guess you're going to tell me!"

"Because you try and figure things out, instead of just letting them happen."

I sat back in my seat.

"It is not on purpose that we met, and neither was it an accident that I accompanied you to Arizona. I believe that you are in my life for a reason."

Now I was sitting straight up again. "I'm shocked to hear you say that. I mean you have acted so distant since we came back. I didn't know what to think," I explained.

"I want to apologize for that. I want you to know that when I shared my feelings for you in Arizona, I really meant that. It's just that the closer we get to this charity event the more I miss my wife. I guess I kind of felt guilty for allowing myself to like another woman. I'm okay during the entire year. I'm doing fine taking care of Istas. But when I get ready to step on that stage, all the memories of my wife's beautiful smile come back as I remember the last time she stepped onto the stage with me."

I watched as his eyes became glossy as we sat in the silence of the moment. He continued.

"We were supposed to do so much together. We had plans to take over the studio and start this great program. I mean she was such a dreamer. I loved her for that because she challenged me. But then our dreams ended when she got sick with cancer and died."

"So is that why you aren't taking over your mother's studio?" I asked.

"I just didn't think I could do it… I didn't want to do it alone. I almost gave up dancing all together because it was just too hard to go there without her. But one day, I felt strongly in my heart that giving up on dancing would be giving up on her and her dreams. So I started the charity event in her honor and all the ticket sales are donated to the cure."

"Wow, that is inspirational. I guess I didn't realize that you have been through so much. It seems like you are always so strong. I ask for your forgiveness if I have been selfish," I said.

"No need to apologize anymore to me, Truly. It just seems like you expect people to let you down. Knowing what you've been through, I see why you use that as a defense. But I want you to know that it is not my intention to hurt you. I mean everything I say to you."

Mark drove me back to my car. He escorted me to my car, my mind had hundreds of thoughts happening at the same time, my heart beating a thousand times a minute it seemed. He grabbed the handle of my car door then opened his arms wide for a hug. I fell into his embrace and we hugged for what seemed to be only seconds, leaving me longing for it to have been longer. He kissed me gently on the forehead before I got into my car.

By the end of the night, I finally could see that things were working on my behalf. I just had to be willing to wait. When I got home, before going to bed, I opened my journal, dated it Saturday, December 8, 2012, to write one word:

"Content."

Staring at the page I flipped back to the night before, Friday, December 7, 2012 which read: "I think I'm starting to like Steven. This last date was really great."

I slammed my journal closed, "Oh gosh what am I going to do?"

Over the past week, I talked to Cynthia every day, who invited me to stay with her in Arizona until I found a place. I didn't tell her I had enough money saved, thanks to my Dad, to pay for over six months of rent, but I wanted to allow life to just take me where it wanted for a change. I landed a part-time job at a dance camp teaching children. I also planned to enroll in school to further my career in dance. Mark and I spent several days together getting to know one another. Although we were not an official couple, I felt the dancing butterflies one feels inside when they are in the newness of a potential relationship. As this wonderful bliss was happening in my life, there was this constant ill-feeling I was carrying with me because I still had to break it off with Steven.

I was lying on the couch when my phone rang. I picked it up and it was Steven. I stared at the screen until it read "*Missed Call.*" For the past week, I would just ignore the call due to feelings of guilt that wouldn't allow me to break it off with him. Tonight I felt it was time. I excused myself from the living room and went to my room.

"Hello."

"Hi Steven, it's Truly."

"I know who this is and you have been avoiding me."

"I know, I have just been busy."

"Truly what's really going on? One minute we are having a good time, and all of a sudden you are busy. You know you can be honest," he said.

"You're right. I think the real reason why I started hanging out with you in the first place is that I was in a vulnerable place in my life, and I am sorry."

There was silence then the sound of the dial tone.

The day of the winter recital finally arrived. I woke up very excited to see how months of preparation would be on display at tonight's show. After showering, I went downstairs to the kitchen to eat, Pamela was placing some bowls of breakfast food on the table, "Good morning Truly. It's your big day!" she said.

"Um, my big day? More like Vanessa's. Remember, I am the understudy. Matter of fact, where is she?" I asked.

"She ran to the store to get some orange juice. Somebody forgot to add it to the list." she said, pointing to my dad as he walked in.

"Good morning honey, it's your big day," he said, kissing me on the cheek before grabbing a napkin and sitting at the table.

I sat down next to him, "You guys are all acting very weird."

They just laughed. Shortly, Vanessa came in with the orange juice and we all ate breakfast. I talked to them about my moving to Arizona. Surprisingly, both my Dad and Pamela gave me their blessing and promised to visit once I got settled.

For the rest of the afternoon, I pretty much hung around the house relaxing in my room. I packed a few small things that I didn't need at the moment. I pulled out a box from my dresser, upon opening it, I found the small cards from Mark that were given to me when he left me the roses. I smiled as I read each one before closing the box and placing them in a bigger box that I planned to tape up soon.

Evening came and I went downstairs to let my parents know I was heading to the auditorium. I wanted to ask them where Vanessa was, thinking we could ride together, but no one was home.

I got to the auditorium and it was just as beautiful as the first time I saw it, except there was additional lighting, decorations, and double the stage crew hustling around to help this event be a success. I went to the back of the stage and pushed open a door with a sign that read, "Performers and Backstage Crew Only," and there was Lily.

"Tonight is your big night," she said, snatching me close for a hug then pulling me face to face. She was grinning from ear to ear. Her hair was tied back in a beautiful bun. I thought to myself, *she is so beautiful*, but what came out of my mouth was, "Why does every-one keep saying that?! I am just the understudy!"

"Oh, so they haven't told you yet, oops," she said, covering her mouth.

"Tell me what?" My confusion turned into a slight bit of worry because I didn't know what to do with my confusion. Lily took me by the hand and guided me a short distance. She instructed me to go back to the make-up room where Vanessa was. I hesitantly followed her directions. I entered into this large room that was covered with large, bright lights surrounding large mirrors. People were in costume and getting their make-up on. There was Vanessa standing at a make-up mirror with Pamela standing next to her. I looked at Vanessa and she had no make-up or costume on. Pamela smiled at me and walked out of the room. She came back with Lily, who then asked all the dancers and make-up artists to briefly leave the room. She closed the door and there was no one left there but Vanessa, Pamela, and myself.

"What's going on? Why aren't you dressed?" I asked Vanessa.

"I'm not dancing the solo with Mark tonight; you are."

My mouth dropped open, "I-I don't understand. Why? What happened?"

"Nothing has happened, other than I realized that what I did, auditioning for this part to get back at you, was evil and wrong. I did it impulsively and not thinking. That guy was not the one for me and that's why he acted the way he did. But instead of blaming him, I took it out on you. I decided several weeks ago that I was not going to dance this solo. I've searched my heart over time, and now I am stepping down. This dance is for you, Truly."

I just stood there looking at the both of them. Pamela began to speak, "Truly, I know that there is nothing Vanessa and I could ever do to take back all the evil that we have done against you, but we can start by admitting we were wrong and asking for your forgiveness."

I stared at Vanessa and Pamela in disbelief. My disbelief turned into concern which made me turn to Pamela, "Why... why don't you like me?" I asked, almost to tears.

She walked over to me and hugged me, "Sweetie, it was never you. It was my own insecurity that drove me to be bitter. I saw how much you made your dad happy after we adopted you. It actually made me jealous. I felt so stupid and like a failure as a wife after we found out I couldn't have any more children for him. Your father never ever faulted me for that. But I chose to carry that shame in my own heart, and it got so out of control I appeased my shame by treating you wrongly because you made your dad so happy. I was wrong. Can you find it in your heart to please forgive me?" she asked, sobbing.

Both she and Vanessa were crying uncontrollably. I hugged Pamela, and Vanessa came over and joined us, sandwiching me between them. "I forgive you," I told the both of them.

"Girl, okay we've got to get going here, you have a show to do tonight," Vanessa said.

They left the room, and I put on my costume. I looked at myself in the large mirror with the white leotard and tutu on. I sat down in the make-up chair, sobbing uncontrollably. This time not because I was sad, hurt, mad, or confused. I cried joyfully because I made it through my test. Things were now working for my good. A few moments later there came a soft knock at the door. I grabbed a tissue and cleaned up my face,

"Come in," I shouted. In walked Mark.

"Hey, I just talked to your family and they told me they told you. How do you feel?" he asked.

"So, you knew?"

"Yeah, they came to me several weeks ago and asked me. Of course I didn't mind. But they wanted to tell you, that was very important to them. So I swore to keep it a secret," he said, raising his hand indicating he made a promise.

"I would have never known. You are a good secret keeper," I said, laughing.

I stood up to meet him as he walked closer to me. I felt the butterflies in my stomach start dancing again. I felt the warmth of his body as he came close to me. Before he came close briefly because there were boundaries keeping us apart. Not this time, no boundaries or limits. He grabbed me by my waist and pulled me into his body. It didn't seem like he was planning on letting me go soon. I rested my arms on his shoulders, staring into his eyes. I laid my head on his chest. I was where I was supposed to be, in his embrace. He took his hand placing it softly under my chin lightly lifting my head. He looked into my eyes,

"I haven't been this close to anyone in a long time," he said.

I gave him a soft smile before his eyes shut pushing his lips close to mine. I met him half way with a kiss. I wanted him to know I wanted this just as much as he did. We embraced. We kissed.

He gently pulled me away again to look into my eyes.

"I wanted to know if you would make it official and be with me. Will you be my girlfriend?" he asked.

I said, "Yes." Of course.

We giggled together and talked about how excited we were to do this show together before Lily came in with the make-up artist and the hairstylist to help me finish getting ready. I stared at myself in the mirror as they fixed my hair and dressed my face. I looked very beautiful when they finished, but when I looked in the mirror I saw that the beautiful radiance had been in me all along. It existed a part from the makeup, the costume, even the solo with Mark. Flowing from me tonight was faith in God. I realized God was working His plan for my life all along. Taking the hand of my Beanie, walking onto the stage with him that night I knew no matter the weapon formed against me in Christ, I still prosper.

# Epilogue

*Istas,*

*It is December 2, 2016, and I can't believe this day has finally come, and I am giving this to you. Last night, you asked your dad and I how we met. We weren't ignoring you when we told you that we would talk about it later. We knew this day would come.*

*Your dad and I discussed how we would tell you how we got married and took over Grandma's studio because one day you would be ready and ask. I prepared this journal for you because as you now know, I know how it feels to be adopted, just as I have adopted you. I want you to hide Jeremiah 29:11 in your heart. This will help you to remember you are unique and special. When you read it know that God has a plan for your life. Never compare yourself to others. You are beautiful and special just as you are.*

*I wanted to give you something special. I want you to see everything that I went through that helped shape my faith in God and built my character as a woman. I can testify that God has been, and always will be there for me. No matter how you are feeling remember God is for you. If you ever have doubt about yourself and your existence, you can know with confidence that God was, is, and will always be there for you, too.*

*Yours,*
*Truly*

## About the Author

Crystal White has received a Master of Arts in Mental Health Counseling from MidAmerica Nazarene University, and she received a Bachelor of Arts degree in Interpersonal and Public Communication from the University of Missouri - Kansas City. Crystal is a member of the American Counseling Center and focuses on faith-based counseling.

"My future career goal is to work in an outpatient community center for 2 years post graduation. After becoming a licensed clinical professional counselor, I eventually want to open up a women's shelter that will provide counseling, job resources, and spiritual care until a job and housing is secured by the recipients of the services."

Crystal and her husband Anthony, along with their son, live in Kansas City.

To catch up on Crystal's future projects and events, go to shininglikeyou.com